Canicule

Louis Armand

EQUUS

BY THE SAME AUTHOR

FICTION
The Garden
Menudo
Clair Obscur
Breakfast at Midnight

POETRY
Séances
Erosions
Inexorable Weather
Land Partition
Malice in Underland
Strange Attractors
Picture Primitive
Letters from Ausland
Synopticon (with John Kinsella)

CRITICISM
Incendiary Devices
Techne
Solicitations
Literate Technologies
Event States

CANICULE

LOUIS ARMAND

© Louis Armand, 2013
Cover image: Libor Fára, *Poloha snící akvabely* / z cyklu *Snídaně o půlnoci* / 1950
© the Estate of Libor Fára & the National Gallery, Prague

ISBN 978-0-9571213-3-1

Equus Press
Birkbeck College (William Rowe)
43 Gordon Square, London, WC1 H0PD, United Kingdom

Typeset by lazarus
Printed in the Czech Republic by PB Tisk

Composed in 11pt Garamond, based on type designs by the 16th century punch-cutter Claude Garamond, with headings in Univers Condensed, composed in 1954 by Adrian Frutiger, & Futura Light, composed in 1927 by Paul Renner.

CANICULE

for Clare & Natascha
& in memory of Robert Andrew Ostle

1
synchronicity

The question isn't to paint something altogether different from a man, a house, a mountain, but to paint a man who resembles a man as little as possible – a house that preserves of a house exactly what's needed to reveal the metamorphosis – a cone miraculously emerging – as a snake from his slough – from what used to be a mountain.

– José Ortega y Gasset

An indigent men's boarding house: a small airless room in half-light. Man, bare-chested, pacing the narrow strip between bed, wardrobe, washstand. After however many turns, he comes to a stop in front of the wardrobe. Opens it. Removes a petrol tin from a shelf. Shuts wardrobe. Returns to pacing, now sprinkling petrol around the room as he goes. Sits on edge of bed. With his free hand draws blankets around his shoulders. Douses them with petrol. Drops the empty tin on the floor. Takes out a packet of matches. *Safety matches.* Lights one. The room ignites...

Between opening credits, fade in on: A flashing orange light. A street-cleaning truck late at night in a city. Neon sign over the entrance to a bar. The name doesn't matter...

Interior, bar scene: *Wild is the Wind* playing on a jukebox. A man asleep at the bar, empty glass in front of him. Barman grabs his shoulder, shakes him.

"Hey, your name Hess?"

Man comes awake startled. Stares at the empty glass like he's lost something.

"Who says?"

"Call for you."

Barman jerks a thumb at a wall-phone at the end of the bar. Man turns the empty glass in his hand, in a way you might describe as thoughtful.

"Same?" Barman.

Man says: "Yeah. Make it the same…"

Telephone: a woman's voice in the receiver.

"You didn't call."

"How'd you know I was here."

"A little birdie."

"Been a while."

"That was your choice."

"Good to be back."

"Bullshit. You could never wait to get out of there."

"You hated this place as much as I did."

"You're not the one who was married to it."

"What d'you want me to say? I'm sorry? Okay, I'm sorry."

"You're not sorry."

"You're right, I'm not."

"Wolf tell you what happened?"

"He told me to call you…"

"And you didn't."

"You got my message."

"Ascher's dead, Hess."

"I know…"

❁

Black sand stretches away as far as the humid mind's eye can see. Branching, in the middle distance, an inky channel flows north to the sea, flanked by tidal flats. Sheets of greasy water in which heron stand, thin, grey, calligraphic. The longer you look, the greyer they become, drawn shapes bleeding at the edges, contrast dialled down to zero. To the left, a strip of shaly beach slopes into the water, fringed with pines, grassed dunes where the broken ends of stormwater drains vent their discard. A saturated, estuarine smell lingers in hot unshifting air like sex or effluent. Reminding of wet concrete floors in public shower blocks. Grey-white flowers loll above reeds & spear grass, casting no shadows. Across the sandbar, seagulls swoop at a carcass exposed by the surf, chased away by a yapping mutt.

In the reality of the present, it's just after three a.m. The remembered scene unspools in black-&-white, synchronous with the erratic streetlight outside the window. I'm lying on a hotel bed, plotting the end of a story whose moral escapes me. It's a story I've spent too long trying to remake or forget but it won't relent. Sound familiar? Wanting the past to be a blank space that can be filled with anything, when you know all those stuffings are just a type of forgery. Well, who cares if a man hates himself.

In the unreality of memory, it's midsummer, twentyfive years ago. I'm standing just outside that scene with the sea at low ebb, the dunes behind & glimpses of houses between the dunes. In the foreground, a boy, short blond hair, lying facedown in black waterlogged sand, unmoving. Misshapen adolescent body aglow. Playing dead. He lies unbreathing, waiting for something to happen. A woman, large dark sunglasses & knit bikini, enters the frame. Squats. Wrenches the boy over onto his back. Still playing dead, face blackened with sand. A telltale erection's visible through cotton bathing shorts as the woman slaps him. Stupid little shit, she says. Voice in time delay. Echoing. A voice underwater. The boy laughs, doing nothing to evade the woman's blows. Her anger spent, the boy frees himself & runs away across the tidal flat into the glimmering light, flapping his arms as if they were wings.

The tiny figure recedes further & further till I can barely make him out. He's disappearing. The water, the sand, the shale-strewn beach are also disappearing. I can't hang onto them. Were they ever as real as they seemed just now?

Fade from black-&-white to desaturated colour. Seventies kodachrome. A hotel room, the décor three decades old. A bed. A man, fully dressed, lying there on his back. Close-up on the face. Black around the eyes, cheekbones sticking out. Yellowish. Well, I was never what you'd call pretty. Unslept for how long? The journey. Insomnia. And before all that... Was there ever a *before all that?* This wasn't one of the endings I had in mind. Does it make a difference how I look at things from now on? Here's an alternative scenario – tell me if you reckon it's any better...

❂

Scene: Man gets up & crosses the room to a small writing desk in front of a window & switches on a lamp (in these words exactly, narrating his own actions to himself). Lying there, on the desk, is a black leatherbound notebook. The man looks at it. It seems different to when I look at it. Focus on that.

The notebook: I used to try to record ideas in it, for a film I eventually realised I was never going to make. Then it simply became a repository – for scraps, pieces of evidence to prove the inner life hadn't yet completely withered away.

Focus on the man reaching for the notebook & opening it, turning the pages. July, on the underside of Europe, three months ago: *Die Welt ist fort, ich muß dich tragen.* The world's gone, I've got to carry you. Who said that? The man thumbs through the notebook at random: *Beneath us the sky was like a slab, shimmering under water.* His finger slips down the page, tracing the ends of the lines. Further on: *Tonight I dreamt of the perfect film. A*

12

film about three characters whose lives are completely empty. Or fictitious in the sense of concealing the absence of a real existence. Or simply unreal, static, made up of nothing. I woke & tried to write the dream down. Its actual situations. But only ended up with fragments of description.

Like a punchline without a joke…

Who thinks that, me or him? Outside it's raining – the bay's invisible in the darkness beyond the marina. I see the words the man's been reading dissolve in front of me & in their place a faint red light hovering. The taillight of the ferry to Göteborg. Larvik. Trelleborg. The container ships plying the Kieler Förde. The red light's blinking obsessively & the words in my mind begin to blink also.

❂

But why not tell it like it really is? Begin with that much, keep in the margins, let the story speak for itself. The full two reels' worth. You can save the tears for the curtain act. This's no reminiscence. All I've got are images, I try to crack them open to see if anything's living inside. Meanwhile, up there on the big screen, the sweep & flicker of headlights scrawl their mind-mandalas. And me down here. Stuck. As always, trying to decipher impenetrable things. Out of fear of the obvious. It doesn't matter that none of this'll ever add up, it isn't supposed to. Perhaps the moral's knowing the difference between telling a story & describing one. Or knowing what a story is & what it isn't.

I get up. I go to the desk & stand in the place the man was standing. Already the room looks different. Question: What'd I come back here for, after staying away so long? Pick up the notebook. Open it. Turn the page. More of the same: *Why shouldn't it just be possible to begin & go on without the necessity, at every moment, of holding yourself in check?* The dog stalking at the back of

13

the mind. Do I expect to find an answer this way? Pretending, not-pretending. And then I come to the entry that started all of this. Friday, 14 July: *Message from W that A's dead.*

Ascher. Head shaved. Scars under his eyes. A stiffened mask-like face. And that ridiculous name, predestining him. What was he now but another of those inconvenient fictions we carry around with us. Constantly repairing. Editing. Re-casting. Making grotesque the more we worry it. He'd been nothing, while he lived. An artist. What the hell's an artist? None of us had eyes for what he'd suffered. Like his art. Sketched with gestures that always sought but never attained resolution. As disappointed & portentous as that.

But Ascher had no ambition to be anything other than what he was & I envied him for it. I envied him because I couldn't hold him. He slipped away. The way a part of you slips away because you can't look at yourself without hating what you see.

Maybe that's why, when I think back, it isn't Ascher but Wolf who always comes to mind. As a moment ago, there on that beach where we lost whatever passed then for innocence. Wolf whose voice on the phone was weighted with accusation: *You should've done something.* I mouth the words. What was I supposed to've done? You stir the conscience a little. People still die, in spite of us.

Ask why. Demand something. A response. An alibi. Why not the whole song & dance as well? Life's messy. Unlike in films. Things happen just the way they do, for no reason.

Once upon a time someone, I can't remember who, said sooner or later we pay with years of sorrow for every moment of happiness. Time turns into a cave whose mouth's blocked. We grope through the claustrophobia towards that one, failing light. Is it the light at the end, or an hallucination? A retinal defect, or a glint in the eye of the inner beast waiting in its lair? Who ever really believed the idea that time reveals a secret design, rather than moving towards emptiness & deadness?

But who am I trying to kid?

Is that why you came back? To lay your own nonsense to rest?

The bedside clock reads 3:46. I know I'll never get to sleep this way. If I lie down I'll just stare at the ceiling all night. What's left of it. Four hours roughly till the zero hour: Wolf. I decide to take two of Luce's "suicide pills" (Nembutal) to force the issue & wonder how many it'd actually take to kill someone.

❁

Did Ascher spare himself any of the pain at the end? Why would he? Pain was all he had left. Living on the skids, in a doss house for indigents down by the Kiel navy yards. *The Rex.* King of the world. His last year, drifting in circles, from one desperation to the next. Marita swore he'd gone crazy. Certified crazy. Right over the edge. He stalked their kids. She petitioned a magistrate to have him put away. There was a warrant, Wolf said. I pictured Ascher locked down in a cell. Shaved head. Bare-knuckled in solitary with only a shitcan & voices through the air-ducts. Then tried to picture him on the outside, hiding-out, spiralling ever deeper. How long before the end became an inevitability? He gave no sign, left no note. The world didn't deserve as much. One day he simply doused himself with petrol & lit a match.

2
Notre Dame des Anges

A long low drawn-out tenor saxophone E-flat purrs in the hot night air. It curls through shadowed backstreets behind the Boulevard du Boramar, the rue Saint-Vincent, the rue Pasteur, the Place du 18 Juin with coloured lanterns strung from balcony railings & tree branches crisscrossing the square. Drunken shouts follow along the strand towards the Place d'Église & out onto the breakwater. Revellers leap & dive, splashing in the dark beneath a low stone ledge jutting from the rounded steeple of Notre Dame des Anges. Soon voices can be heard approaching the shore where carnival lights dance across the water, around the wild bodies.

In the Place du 18 Juin, a woman in an emerald green dress was dancing in front of an improvised bandstand, arms swaying as she turned & turned like a boutique mannequin on a rotating pedestal, which'd almost been brought to life. A mannequin with its head tilted back, eyes closed, trailing waves of auburn hair & laughing, a weird laughter from deep down in its throat. The long note hung on & reached a new plateau, pitched between a moment's ecstasy & dénouement. A drum rim, a bass riff, & the music broke once more into a syncopated frenzy like the death throes of a dying machine. Voices rose up as the woman turned faster then faster still, keeping tempo with the jazz. The drifting crowd awoke briefly from its torpor & milled around, watching, expectant, suddenly on edge. Then just as abruptly the music came to an end, the coloured lights faded-out & the streets emptied for the few remaining hours before dawn. Waiters from the café-bars stacked away chairs & swept up, their movements sketched in faint outline against the surrounding shadows. Below the terraces, the last small remaining groups sat drinking wine from bottles, forsaken by the rest of their tribe. A swollen moon hung over them like a hole in the night.

The woman in the green dress stood on the beach at water's edge, sandals dangling from her hand. Vacantly she stared. At a piece of broken glass glinting in the moonlight. At anything. She thought: *La lune, la lune.* Cold water inched over her feet. Her ankles. Inching & receding. *Like hands.* Hundreds of them. Thousands. Stretching up beneath the dark sea. Soon she'd be in their grasp. There'd be no escape.

The green glass glimmered, then was washed away.

The woman's mood turned desolate. Something shapeless, indefinable, yet there. Indisputably *there.* Separated from the music she felt like a thing. Like a stone, a piece of glass. A stone & glass & hands & the cold seawater.

❂

Inside her head an argument was going on & on about nothing – the woman in the green dress. Then she was in a street, walking away from the harbour. A street, the harbour, the sound of footsteps. She searched to get her bearings, to recall a route already travelled. *Where's everybody?* Then: *I'm lost?* She found herself wandering beneath the Miradou. A maze of narrow lanes, stairways, alleys, thinking: *You walk into a dream from certainty to the unascertained?* Those were Hess's words. *From certainty to the...* Then, aloud to herself:

"You're drunk."

Many wrong turns, false leads, hesitations, before recognising

18

at last the way to the hotel. She retraced her steps. Approaching an archway she heard a low murmuring of voices. Two figures in silhouette stood out into the street, barring the way. Before fear, before any thought at all, she was trapped between them, hustled into the dark recess of a doorway. A picture-frame of hanging gardenia. There was no way to resist. Her head swam, she couldn't breathe. Beneath the green dress now wrenched up above her thighs she was naked. Later she'd remember, in the midst of it, saying to herself: *If you scream it'll be worse?* In the blackness of her mind all passed slowly, then very fast.

As the footsteps receded, she squatted in the doorway, the faceless men's semen dripping out of her. She knew from the pain that she was bleeding. The air in the street pressed in hot & humid, pungent with cats' piss & the smell of flowers. If she thought at all, she tried not to. What was there to think? Through gritted teeth a type of snarl: *They stuff it in you & you thank them out of shame for not leaving you dead?*

"Haaaaa," she keened.

Time passed. In her mind everything was already abstracted. What disturbed her most was the smell of them. Pastis, sweat & cheap cologne. It clung to her like...

She exhaled as hard as she could, till her lungs spasmed & she drew in, hand over mouth. Realising her eyes were still shut, she started, like someone suddenly awake. Then, regaining some part of her composure, fumbled out a handkerchief & wiped herself. Slowly, hesitant, rose to her feet. Dimly the shapes of rote thoughts stood out. An inner voice, speaking with a detachment reminiscent of a school mistress, who when she was seven lectured them on *practical matters.* There was, she instructed herself, a clinic in Argelès. *I'll go in the morning? Later. In the morning.* Of course, they'd want to do tests. They'd ask questions. And all at once the whole miserable effrontery of her predicament appeared before her. Doctors. Gendarmes.

Embassy officials. Her publisher in Paris. Hess... *No! Say nothing.*
Forget it ever happened. Do you even know what happened? What would
you tell any of them? They'll say, "You were drunk?" "You did something
to encourage them?" "You didn't say no?"

In the distance, a sound like laughter. Echoing. Distorted.
Heia lala... Her thoughts stopped. From a balcony above, a cat
mewed, plaintive. Then with conscious effort the woman
breathed deeply again & exhaled, all the while staring straight in
front of her. As her breathing became regular, she impatiently
readjusted her dress, the strap of her handbag. And then, as
though in a delayed action, she doubled over & vomited.

❂

The hotel was completely in darkness. As she stood at the door,
the woman in the green dress studied her reflection in the glass
panes & combed her hair from her face with her fingers. She
knew she was trembling but tried not to look at her hands as she
mistyped, repeatedly, the security code. Inside, she unhooked a
key from the board behind the unattended reception desk &
started, with slow deliberate steps, up the narrow stairway. At the
second landing she hesitated, peering at one door & then the
next, their numbers playing tricks in the dark. Aware of the
sound her own breathing made, she held her breath & found
herself gasping, on the verge of panic.

Then the corridor echoed with the sound of keys being
fumbled & a lock turning, & she was standing in a room bathed
in moonlight, the shadows of leaves stirring on an unmade bed.
In the far corner of the room she could distinguish the shape of
a person sitting in an armchair, the glint of eyes signalling that
she was being watched. For a moment she stood still, staring
across the room at those eyes, attempting to draw out of the
shadows the face of the one she expected to find. A younger

woman's flat, emotionless voice:

"Louise?"

"Yes."

"I heard you coming up the stairs."

"Yes," she said.

"You weren't with him?"

"No."

"I waited."

"Yes."

"No. Yes. Isn't there something else you can say?" A note of distress crept into the other's voice.

"You could've stayed," she said finally.

"I was tired. I couldn't bear it. I didn't feel well."

The one called Louise crossed the room to where the other was sitting in the shadows, in an open dressing-gown. She stood beside the chair.

"But you're better now," she said, trembling slightly while caressing the younger woman's hair.

"My God!" the younger woman recoiled. "I can smell him on you!"

"It isn't..."

"Stop it! You're lying. You treat me like a child."

The woman called Louise withdrew her hand. An unreal silence filled the room, which in a moment was broken by violent sobs. Outside a gust of wind set the shadows of a tree moving around the room.

"Why can't you leave me alone!"

A rising note of despair followed her as she closed the door & rushed back through the dark along the corridor. Momentarily she hesitated, as if searching for something among the doors at the far end of the landing. Then she rushed down the stairs & left the hotel. Except for the patter of a stray dog stalking towards the cemetery, the street was deserted. A faint greyness had begun to tinge the sky above the hills.

As she approached the parking lot, the woman realised she was no longer carrying her sandals. She thought: *I've left them upstairs?* But she knew she must've lost them on the way from the beach. She closed her eyes. *Why should I care about a pair of sandals?* And all of a sudden a convulsive, formless emotion overwhelmed her. She lurched through the parking lot towards the safe haven of her car. An echo of the younger woman's sobbing filled her ears as she slumped into the driver's seat. Winced. Turned the ignition. The noise of the engine drowning everything else out.

❂

The white convertible sped through the predawn. Headlamps radiating in the gloom as a clash of gears filled the air. The woman in the green dress jerked the steering wheel through a rapid series of hairpins. Vague outlines flashed past, weirdly animate. *Louise.* Her name. She remembered that much. *And what if you could undo it all?* she thought. *Abolish it? Strike it from the face of the earth?* The car skidded, sending up dry clouds of dust as it pulled out of the last corner & accelerated along the narrow ridge. A black scar across the landscape marked the recent path of a forest fire. The sour ash-pit smell still clung to the air.

Up ahead the road veered down to Port-Vendres. Easing off, she let the car coast up to the silhouette of Fort St-Elme, its round-tower a blinded lighthouse on a blackened rock. She nosed the car off the road into a clearing & stalled the engine. Immediately a heavy silence fell. Out of it gradually came the ticking of the hot metal beneath the bonnet. The flare of a cigarette lighter illuminated the woman's face, replaced by the orange glow of a cigarette. Time passed while she sat there, smoking cigarette after cigarette. The sky changed colour behind the old fortress, its hulk little by little diminishing against the reddening smoke-haze.

She tossed the butt of her last cigarette on the ground & climbed from the car. Straightening her dress, she walked barefoot across the clearing & followed a dirt path through the low scrub to a ledge that stood out like a proscenium. Behind her the silhouette of the Albères massif, shrouded in smoke, loomed against the sky. A breath of wind whispered in the tops of the trees. Below was stillness. The between-tides. Through a thin film of angry tears she stared down at the village of Collioure & at the long faint curve of the coastline towards Perpignan. Like a cicatrix on the sea.

Without knowing why, she said to herself: *You have to go as far as you know you should. Life. Art. No excuses. No... justifications.* Immediately she thought of Hess. What would she say when she got back? He'd look into her eyes & she'd say... But the thought wouldn't complete itself. *Cut them with a knife! Castrate them! It's your fault!* She began to cry uncontrollably. Her ravaged face, streaked with mascara. A smear in place of a mouth. *Why weren't you there?* Then: *Damn you! It's your own stupid fucking fault. Why couldn't you've just waited?*

And as she stared half-blind at the sea, daybreak came suddenly over the water. A rose-tinted haze low in the East. Against the brazed hillside. The tiny façades abutting the port, bathed in ochreous light.

3

celluloid

Les lumières sont très fortes, les
ombres très claires. L'ombre est tout
un monde de clarté et de luminosité
qui s'oppose à la lumière du soleil,
ce qu'on appelle des reflets.
— André Derain

Somebody dies & right before your eyes they turn to celluloid. Is
that all there is? Accumulations of mental snapshots. Fragmented
points-of-view from a film long ago buried in the vaults. Out-
cuts waiting to be spliced together again, always pointing to
some missing reel. The one in which all the scenes magically
connect. Never to see the light of day...

Another migraine's working its meticulous way up the back
of my neck, into the space behind my left eye. Hands all pins &
needles. Waiting for the lights to streak through my head. If I
think about it too long, maybe I'll hyperventilate. Since Ascher
died, three months ago, the frequency of the headaches has only
increased. I've taken it as a signal that deep inside something
knows & is grieving on my behalf. Causing me at least to suffer.
I've felt the fever of all these things fighting, but the migraine
itself is impenetrable. Indecipherable.

I tell myself to go beyond it, write it down. But when I
actually get around to writing, there're only fragments. Nothing
coheres. The words flicker. An empty signal. A failed Morse
dissolving in the fog behind the eyes, where thought ceases &
pain begins. It's easy to indulge in the idea that it's a form of
punishment. Some God, tyrant, nobodaddy, standing over me

25

with pointed finger. Credulous enough to believe I'm unable even to tell my own story. Standing on a precipice, looking down into the abyss of things that used to be sensible, once had a function, a meaning, or were merely there. And in their place, nothing. Only gibberish. Words spiralling in their own noise.

✪

Before he embarked for Beirut, Wolf made some remark probably intended as a bit of wisdom to help me on my way, but which just sounded pretentious. Like the parting shot of a smartarse in a film who thinks they're stealing the scene:

"Memory doesn't exist. The *past*, doesn't exist. It *never* existed. Everything we see behind us or ahead of us is a dream. The world, us in it, *history*, is exactly as precarious as this."

And if we should awaken, would we drown? In the notebook I come across an entry which says: *We scan the headlines. A family of 7 killed in the latest bombardment at Gaza Beach. Who's to blame? 400th anniversary of Rembrandt's birth. In 400 years, what'll be remembered about this day? (No justice in commemoration.)* Wolf's voice in my head: *You don't believe in the divine right of kings, so why believe in the divine right of nations?* Mankind *has no right to exist…*

Another entry of the same day, 14 July: *The tiniest fragment breathes forth its connection to everything else. The unknown under the surface of the water. A suppressed thought about to return, threatening to return, having already returned. Am I, too, in the business of impersonating myself? Item: A red & white striped carousel marquee, surmounted by a rearing horse in a green harness. Children riding this anachronism. Item: A clown performing on the beach, just below the terrace, juggling imaginary objects in front of a captivated audience. Magic is real…*

What's any of this got to do with my being here? Using Wolf as an alibi, once again backing away from the light, withdrawing into my cave. As I expected, the Nembutal was no use. In a little while I'll go down & get some coffee at the diner across the street. Maybe some breakfast, though I'm not hungry. A picture of watery coffee, eggs & Matjeshering. Rollmops, potato salad, Braten – all those childhood horrors. Outside, the October drizzle shimmers against the neon. Not so far from here, near the marina, is the place Wolf used to live, alone with his mother in a large half-empty house. Both *alone* & *with*. There's a supermarket there now, with a car park along one side. The taxi passed by it last night on the way to this hotel. *Der Schnorchel* or *der Schnörkel*, I can't remember which.

Note to self: Find out what became of Ascher's paintings? But I've no sooner written it down than I crumple it up & throw it on the floor. Why begin now? What Luce would say: There's a wall inside me I can't see past to the other side. The side which's supposed to experience emotions that aren't purely self-centred? What am I supposed to feel? *For the next twentyfour hours / days / months I intend to be sad & exhibit all the appropriate signs of grief.* Going through the motions of absolving oneself.

I'm reminded: Three days ago in Paris, with Luce. It was the opposite of the time in Prague just before Wolf re-entered the picture. The whole thing was tediously banal. Luce had gone to Paris (again), "to find herself." Ada was at loose ends, making a general nuisance of *her*self, waiting, camera in hand, for something to happen. Present in a neglected kind of way, like a woman in a film who's intended to be an enigma simply to be laid bare & infantilised. An inert, passive organism begging for the infliction of pain. Which means, I suppose, that she was already in love with Luce, even then.

So when Wolf came on the scene, full of violence & purpose & intimated vulnerabilities, all of them fake, well... Ada was a sitting duck. Thinking she was revenging herself on Luce. The sacrificial virgin… Frigidity arouses something in a certain kind of male. Like an eroticised paradox. Wolf, on the other hand… Perhaps she reminded him of his mother.

You don't need a shrink to figure how a scene like that'd have to play out. But as the song says, history never repeats. Not if it's the details that matter. The rest? Sure, there's always the big master plan. Right? God watching in the back brain, pulling the strings. Wolf? His story was no different. And just like all these stories, it started with a father.

❂

The legend of Wolf's father began during a plane hijacking, in the Autumn of 1977. The botched execution appeared live on network news. Shot in the neck & left on the tarmac to bleed to death, framed in close-up by a cameraman's telephoto lens. Wolf's mother, an actress in a TV drama, never recovered from the experience of seeing her husband murdered between commercial breaks. Later she attempted suicide. Wolf was five when it happened, but he still remembered what'd been playing in the background on the imported Vistavision TV set (*Hitparade*), what his mother had been wearing (a white Yves Saint Laurent pantsuit), & what brand of rat poison (Neudorff).

The three of us – me, Ascher, Wolf – were sitting under the pine trees one May afternoon, watching the tide reddening in the sunset, when a sombre mood crept over us & Wolf, gaze fixed on the horizon, told us about it. His mother had called him into the kitchen. She'd mixed the rat poison into a glass of milk, drank it, then mixed a second glass, put the other down in front of him & told him to drink it too. He'd tried, but the taste was so bad he couldn't. His mother got angry. She poured sugar into the glass & ordered him to drink. When he gagged, she got so irritated she snatched the glass from his hand & drank it herself. Then she shut herself in the bathroom, came out a few minutes later with lopsided makeup on, started to cry & ran out of the house. Next thing he was at the hospital. Orderlies rushing past. Someone who might've been his mother puking all over herself.

Wolf went to live with relatives in Aachen. Later, when his mother returned from the clinic, they sent him back. Somehow she'd botched it. It didn't bother the rels that maybe the old girl wasn't fit for the job. The kid was a burden. Like a pair of fugitives in a 1940s movie, they fled north to an old run-down summer house near the sea.

And that's how we all came to meet, in the unreality of the long summer of '83. The year the US embassy in Beirut got bombed. The year of the phoney Strategic Defence Initiative some genius dubbed "Star Wars." We still made-believe in Superman, kryptonite, fast-breeder reactors & critical mass. Missile silos & coolingstacks populated the distant exotic landscapes of our imagination. Ronald Reagan & Yuri Andropov danced into the sunset of a world with no future. We cranked up the fat lady's anthem to the closing credits, till the batteries ran flat. Glasnost was half a lifetime away.

Three boys in a fading kodachrome. Ascher, Wolf & me on the right. Head cocked. Indulging in a kind of inscrutability. Each of us with towel & satchel bag, bare ankles & sandshoes, long khaki shorts, dirty knees, shirts hanging out, grinning. Who took that picture? It's almost the opposite of the only other one I've still got from those days. Black-&-white. Standing together in front of a cinema marquee. Hair slicked. Regarding the camera with an air of juvenile insolence. I look in the mirror. Me, my head, my face. Am I still the same person as the kid in those photographs?

Some cryogenic ghost, frozen in time, forever waiting-out the purgatory of adolescence. Pleasant thought. But the faces in those pictures betray nothing of inner emotional lives. They're perfect. Like statues of light composed into a remote & inaccessible geometry.

What were the odds? Fate, we thought. Brought together on that backwater Dogstarland. At the end of the world. Because it was misshapen like us? Growing up there, we never knew how much we hated it. The flatness. The swamp-dog stench & mugging summer heat. The freezing winters. Sometimes what you hate's what you long for most without realising it. Like wanting a father to hate, because you've never had one.

It probably isn't true, but the image I have of when we first met is one of those impenetrable overcast days with grey sky reflected on greyer water. It was vacation time. Time outside of time. Like a long silence waiting for something to creep up on you. Seagulls flocked on the edge of the tidal flat where the channel cut a swathe of dark cross-currents. Halfway out, someone had sunk a wooden stake into the sand through the decomposed remains of a bottle-green jellyfish. Some kind of magnetism drew us to it & we stood there, barely aware of each other's presence. Staring at the trembling mass.

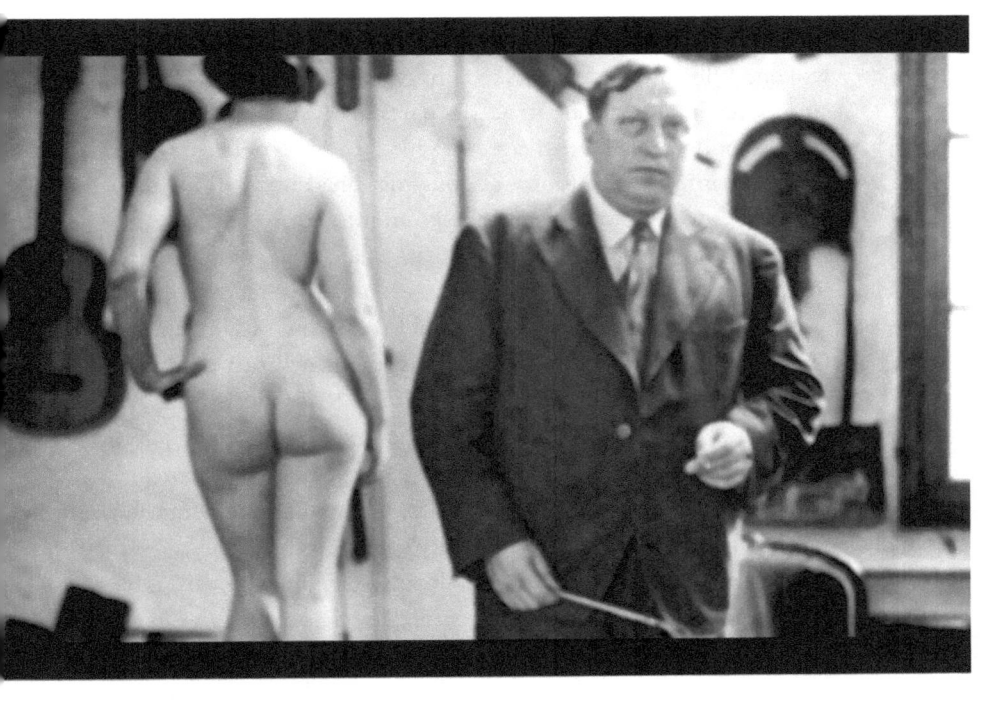

4
Wild Beasts

Hess stood on the balcony of his room & breathed heavily. He'd woken, fully dressed & soaked in sweat, feeling he was being smothered in his sleep. It was a particularly repugnant feeling, like the body of a jellyfish covering his face, its tentacles working their way into his mouth. A viscous mass had invaded his throat till some lower brain reflex retched him into consciousness.

It felt as if the left half of his face was paralysed. He massaged his cheek indecisively. A short distance along the street, past the newsstand, Hess could see a row of zinc chairs & tables had been set out along the pavement in front of the café that stood opposite a parking lot named Place du 8 Mai 1945. There had to be some sort of irony, he thought, about consecrating an expanse of grey-black tarmac, in commemoration of the end of WW2, to the ultimate triumph of mass transit & petroleum. Humanity's new God.

A smattering of people were already seated at the café tables, reading newspapers, drinking coffee, oblivious to the sea of chrome, plastic & enamelled steel spread almost at their feet. Hess grimaced. Looking down at that stupidity made his head ache even more. Yet he craved a drink & longed to be sitting also at one of those tables, unconcerned by all that happened around him. He turned back to the open suitcase that lay on his bed & for a moment considered how much easier it'd be to close it again & just walk away. Catch the eight o'clock to Barcelona. And what then? Every other place would be just the same in some fundamental sense. He knew it. There was no escape. *If I can have a drink & calm down,* he thought, *then I'll be able to figure out what to do next.*

For quarter of an hour Hess struggled at the bathroom sink with soap & razor before taking a cold shower & finally getting dressed. He'd exhausted his supply of headache tablets during the journey. The routine was a familiar one. Travel brought out the worst in him. His one desire was to somehow amputate the pain, which usually involved drinking & more pain. A vicious circle he had no real intention of extricating himself from. It excused him from the need to behave as anything other than the civilised ape humanity was. This, at least, is what he told himself as he regarded his bloodshot doppelgänger in the bathroom mirror.

Back out in the bedroom, he sorted through his suitcase to check he hadn't misplaced anything essential. The very idea caused a wry grin to upset the line of his mouth. *Strip a man to the bare essentials*, he thought, *& what's left but a picture of his disappointments?* A handful of scripts slid onto the bed among the clothes still to be bundled into the wardrobe. Arranged on top of a crumpled linen jacket was a passport, denominations in several currencies, a watch with beige leather band, a cell phone. He glanced at the phone, saw there were no messages, & automatically dialled his agent's number. No connection. *Well that's fucking convenient, isn't it Harry?* He killed the phone & hurled it into the suitcase. Pain shot across his temples & he winced.

At that moment, outside, a car horn blared. A delivery truck was blocking the road & traffic had begun backing up behind it. It wasn't even eight o'clock.

"It'll be fine," he said aloud to himself. "Everything's going to be okay. Just one step at a time."

He straightened himself then crossed to the door linking his room to the one adjoining & quietly opened it. But no-one was there & the bed hadn't been slept in. He recognised the familiar disorder of his wife's papers & notebooks strewn across several chairs & a writing desk. He'd arrived in Collioure late the previous evening. There'd been a key, with a barely legible note in his wife's scrawl, waiting on the reception desk. She hadn't been in her room, so he'd gone down to the waterfront. Failing to find her among the crowds in the streets, he'd wound up with a couple of Argentinians in a tapas bar, drinking rum infusions. Coffee, caramel & something tasting vaguely of turpentine. He couldn't remember much else. The state of the clothes he'd slept in said it all.

It'd become a habit for Hess to think of his wife as a type of enigma with whom he happened at times to live. Luce (her name was Louise, & she was from Brighton, but Hess always called her Luce) was a handsome redhead in her late thirties. Approximately ten years earlier they'd entered into a marriage of less than convenience, the reasons for which presently escaped him. The true nature of their relationship was complicated, though he was vaguely aware he himself was the source of that complication.

❁

The idea had been to rendezvous in Collioure, where Luce was finishing a book about the artist André Derain. Luce, for reasons of her own, seemed determined to resurrect his reputation. Irrationally intent, Hess thought, considering – as she'd been first to admit – of all the major figures of the École de Paris, Derain's was the reputation that'd sunk lowest. Six months previous, in Paris, Luce had undertaken, on the strength of a publisher's advance, to write an overview of the artist's Collioure period. That overview had subsequently grown to a full-length monograph, while resisting all efforts at completion.

Derain, son of a pastry chef, met Matisse in 1900 & five years later the two of them were together in Collioure, tearing up whatever remained of the rulebook on pictorial representation & paving the way for Picasso. The armchair critics called them *Les fauves*. Wild beasts. Barbarians. Fanatics. Communards with paint brushes. There was much irony in the fact of Derain's later reincarnation as a stalwart of classicism & upholder of tradition. After the War, he was branded a collaborator. Wrongly, Luce insisted. In the end, a bitter man, he was run down by a milk truck, or a taxi, or a school bus, in Chambourcy & died, only weeks before Matisse, in utter obscurity.

Hess was unsympathetic. About Derain, he cared nothing. About Derain's art, he cared even less. It spoke only of of an unredeemed way of seeing. An angry nostalgia. The raw colour, the crude application of paint with as much of the canvas left exposed as possible. Pushing towards blankness while still shying from it. A negative theology, of blues, yellows, reds. A dogma of overstated violence. As a gesture it was pure anachronism. As if, to arrive at the present, they'd first had to return to some Altamira of the past. To a brutalism from which, in the end, art itself would fall away. Leaving what? After all, hadn't art become just another servility to ideas?

With the publisher's advance, Luce drove down from Paris & rented a room for the season. Hess agreed to join her later, midsummer. He arrived by train, having travelled almost thirtysix hours, including delays, from Prague to Munich, then from Munich to Lyon. The train had left Lyon at 15:36, taking seven hours & twenty minutes to Narbonne. Then three hours more via Perpignan to Collioure. It'd been a grotesque, absurd journey, solely on account of his fear of flying.

It was just at a time when Hess found himself in the middle of a fight that ended with his script being passed to some other nonentity. He wasn't so much as guaranteed a credit. Eighteen months & twohundred pages evaporated into thin air. At least he hadn't invested any of his own money in the production, though he might've if he'd had any. He toyed with the idea of quitting Prague for good. But there was nowhere else to go. Back to the fatherland? You'd have to be kidding. What was it Vilikovský said? *Even if nobody gives a damn about you in your own land, it doesn't necessarily mean you'll be considered a prophet somewhere else.*

Spending a couple of weeks in the south of France had a certain appeal as a way of sticking his head in the sand & letting the world go fuck itself. His thoughts were evidently on the right track: no sooner had he reserved a ticket than his life veered straight into a cul-de-sac. He was officially broke & not a prospect in sight. His agent, Harry Cohen, a Boston Jew related to some bigwig in LA, always making wisecracks like *he* was in a movie, wasn't cracking wise anymore. The couple of producers he'd met weren't returning his calls. While the secretaries of the ones he hadn't, simply hung up. And as icing on the cake, his landlord gave him notice for being three months in arrears.

It'd all begun with a short film he'd made in the Barrandov back-lots, called *The Rabbi*, about an incest relationship between a Terezín inmate & his daughter, Rosina. The script garnered critical acclaim at a minor European film festival. That led to offers of work on a dozen features. Including the pièce de résistance, the source of all his current woes, a medium-low-budget horror called, for better or worse, *The Chronicle of Doctor Caligari*. Now he couldn't sell a treatment for love or money. *Who the fuck d'you think you are, Jean-Luc Truffaut?* Hell, maybe they were right. Maybe his writing stank. Maybe the world had gone to the dogs. Maybe he should quit with whatever dignity he still had intact.

"C'mon Harry, gimme a break..."

"Look kid, it's supposed to be a schlockfest. You take the notes & figure something out by next week, five grand if they can use it."

Eighteen months & two hundred pages later. It was, to paraphrase someone famous, as if all the wine in Bordeaux had turned to piss. Hess told himself he didn't care, he was indifferent to Bordeaux anyway. He could always go back to something menial, like subtitling, or writing reviews. If they'd take him.

It was in the midst of all this that Wolf cast his shadow once more upon Hess's life. And paid his bills for him.

"What're you writing this crap for anyway?" Wolf grimaced, giving Hess's script the perfunctory once-over. "You'll be lucky they *don't* put your name on it. You should thank them. Ten years in this game & all you've got to show for yourself is this? When're you going to write something people can understand?"

How about, Hess thought, *young wannabe writer living in romantic East European city, scripts a series of brutal sex-crimes targeting wealthy heiresses & then videotapes them in progress. The media dubs him the Camera Killer. Sentenced to life imprisonment, he pens a bestselling memoir & becomes the star of an Oscar-nominated documentary casting him as a working class hero led astray...*

A fortnight later, Wolf left town for Beirut & so, no stomach for the fast road to slasher celebrity, here Hess was, hungover, washed-up, & cut loose in the arsehole of nowhere. He gazed around the room morosely, doing the math on all the wasted hours. *Stick around long enough, genius, & who knows, the world might just fall at your feet.* What the fuck had he been *doing* all this time? And Luce, with her unending, unfinished book about a second-rate dauber. Not to mention their so-called marriage, worse than anything even he could've made up. And now this place. A village with nothing to recommend it but a view that might've been accounted pretty if it wasn't for the tourists clambering all over it, the lethargy & stinking heat. He shook his head. What'd he expected? What'd he come all this way *for*?

Hess dragged his right hand across the bedspread in what, had he been scripting it, he would've described as a *resentful* caress. The tiny knots of roughly woven cotton catching under

37

his fingernails. It reminded him of unsized canvas. A distant memory hovered at the edge of consciousness. And then there was nothing, only the sound of his breathing becoming more laboured, & the now agitated clawing of his fingers. In a sudden, convulsive motion, Hess stood up, ripped the bedspread from the bed & left the room, slamming the door behind him.

❂

Café Sola was already crowded with shift-workers when Hess got down to the street, so he continued along the rue Pasteur towards the Boulevard du Boramar, pausing only briefly to look at the display in the window of the pâtisserie. He tried to dispel his sense of unease by focusing on the thought of how pleasant it'd be to have a drink on the beach-front while watching the sea. Hair of the dog.

The grey-pebbled crescent of the Plage Boramar sloped down into the equally grey lapping waters, darkened by the shadow of Notre Dame des Anges. Except for a couple of elderly women gathering stones at the water's edge, the beach was deserted. Like a stage on which a drama waited to be enacted. Out past the church belfry, the light on the water dazzled white beneath a white curtain of haze.

A street sweeper crossed the strand that ran the length of the beach, where waiters set about raising umbrellas & unstacking chairs on the restaurant terraces, preparing for the day's trade. Workers were stringing tricolour bunting from lampposts for the 14th of July, alongside the carnival lights & flags in Catalonian yellow & red. In the backstreets leading down through the village, aproned men hosed the cobblestones outside the restaurant kitchens. While others, in soiled overalls & rubber boots, shouldered sacks of oysters, mussels, sea snails, trucked in from ports further south. The fishing fleets had long ago moved away from Collioure, which had survived since the War as a minor resort. The San Tropez of the Côte Vermeille, as the brochures said. Though decidedly less *chic*. Less *courant*.

The air along the waterfront was still cool at that hour. A faint breeze blew in, ruffling the bunting & umbrellas. Just as Hess was about to seat himself at a table he recognised, at the far end of the terrace, one of Wolf's castoffs sitting alone reading a newspaper. *My God*, he thought. *Is that who I think it is?* He moved closer to get a better look. *What the hell's she doing here?*

5

geometry

On the other hand, the sequence of
a film gives it a unity in time that is
horizontal &, so to speak,
geographical, whereas time in a
painting, so far as the notion applies,
develops geologically & in depth.
                              – André Bazin

It's comforting to believe everything could always have been different, wrapped in cellophaned happiness. But that doesn't make it true. Beneath a cruel star, we three kings journeyed into this fallen world. 1972. Year of the Rat, of the Munich Olympics & Black September. The year Richard Milhaus Nixon was re-elected president of those United States. The year Fischer beat Spassky & the last Apollo mission came fizzling down to Earth. Did our zodiacs know something we couldn't? Our little destinies written in the twinkley stars? Pascal says: *It's ridiculous to speak of man as if he were a geometrical proposition.* Well then, what kind of proposition *is* a man?

It's almost five o'clock. Time's dragging its feet. There's a telephone sitting on the writing desk, beside the notebook. Black with a knotted cord & push buttons. I keep expecting it to ring any second. It's getting on my nerves. The diner will be opening soon. I want to get out of this room, allow myself the luxury of being bored somewhere else. Why am I so anxious about that phone anyway? It looks dead. Like it belongs in a black bin-bag. In a suitcase with its arms & legs sawn off. If or when Wolf calls, it'll be on my cell phone. That stupid piece of *Star Trek* junk

41

designed to slowly microwave your brain while keeping you plugged into the ether 24/7. That was the agreed plan. He'd call & it'd mean he was on his way. Close. Maybe ten minutes. His number would flash on the screen. I wouldn't answer. Strictly no need. Maybe he thought someone would be monitoring. Maybe there'd be nothing to say.

Perhaps it's the Nembutal, making me neurotic. That telephone. Like a lifeline about to recede. Or better still, tied around my neck. I'm afraid to let it go. If I close my eyes I can at least imagine a smooth transition from the hotel room to the diner. But it's only a feint. Can Wolf know what I'm going through? Playing games with me. Like the phone, pretending to be what it isn't. Always on the verge of ringing. Its purpose to keep me wrong-footed.

❂

Born old into this world, we were anachronisms before our time. Together all in the same shipwreck. Washed up on rotted spars. Waiting for the next tide to come in.

Our ship was an upturned Mercedes someone had tried & failed to drive into the sea. Half-buried in the sand, it lay just short of the pine trees on the north side of the beach. We'd perch there, sweating in the bluish moonlight, watching the distant lightning flash over the Ostsee. Scouring our little world for whatever mirrored us. What we found were ticket stubs for a sideshow that'd done its season run & closed down. One day perhaps a salvage crew would arrive & haul whatever was left to the wrecker's yard. Or else they wouldn't & it'd be left up to the tide to finish its work of interment. A bucket of rust caked with seagull shit.

We figured whatever the future had in store for us was decided the day we met. *Wie drei Tropfen Wasser.* With all the privilege of hindsight, d'you think I know better already? There's stuff for a film in that: The boy-narrator grown into some latter-day Pythagoras-of-the-soul, returns to his childhood home. An all-night vigil in a hotel room. By turns cynical & sentimental. Reliving each moment-to-moment of the group mind. Three friends on a beach. The formative years. All that. Then, having grown old. Older. Taking full measuring of the by-now divided self. Whose parts have led separate existences, detached from the total organism. Yet somehow still bound, fractional, mutually implied. Only because it makes no sense for him to think otherwise.

❂

Once upon a time I too believed I was born through a hole in the substance of the world. Immaculately. The man of celluloid. A vital, mobile individuality. But that crap's strictly for cinema. Tokens at the giftshop. The return to Calvary looped on replay. Like a pacemaker wired backwards into the Zeitgeist. Down on your knees: O *mea culpa! Mea maxima culpa!* Why not just laugh instead? While you've still got the insides to laugh with.

Maybe Ascher was right. Always keep an opt-out clause in the instalment plan. When did it all go wrong? Back then, three kids, like we never had a care in the world. Some sort of paradise. Days combing the tidal flats for clam shells & generally practicing whatever kind of escapism presented itself. Buried ourselves in the sand, daring each other to see who'd hold-out longest as the tide came in. Wolf never flinched, but the sand always washed away & left him lolling on his back like a seal. Rewind. Freeze the frame. Keep him there, still buried up to his neck, only his head visible, like the head of some Orpheus washed-up on a remote, mythological shore. Time, perhaps, would supply the missing lyre & the head would sing.

43

✿

At the south end of the beach caves had formed from large boulders balancing against one another on a rocky outcrop. We hid there from the midday sun & scratched runes on the walls. Totem symbols. The insignia of the tribe. Over the far side of the outcrop was an anchorage for houseboats & smaller yachts. We sometimes staged raids against the houseboat kids. Or if there was nothing else in the offing, Ascher & Wolf would do chopsocky on the beach, kicking & somersaulting about in life-or-death struggle, till the effort wore them out. Or we'd lob sand bombs at the waves, then scatter pell-mell to lie in the caves on the damp pungent sand, spying from the shadows at the couples sunbathing naked on the rocks. Sometimes we'd catch them tossing each other off.

Behind the dunes, we imagined orgies of all sorts taking place. Sunday mornings would find used condoms half-buried in the sand, like shrivelled slivers of fat. The leavings of some strange augury. The dunes, like the caves, had a cloying, damp scent. Like claustrophobia or secrecy. Sometimes we'd sneak inside the boatsheds east of the marina. In one, Wolf unearthed a packing box full of old maps, postcards & porno magazines. There was an icebox with bottles of Flensburger. We drank the beer & sat in the cool dim clutter of outboard engines, winches & spare parts, inhaling the smell of diesel & sump oil.

✿

To break the monotony, we'd ride our bikes down the Strandweg past Laboe to look at the old U-boat or watch the ferries crossing the Kieler Bucht. The strand ran due east to Oldenberg, past beaches with self-deluded names like Kalifornien, Brasilien, Schönberg. We'd sit out on the stone seawalls, the low waves breaking beneath us, conjuring tsunamis or Godzilla rising from the sea with fiery breath.

The only cinema in Laboe looked like it could've been a church hall, once upon a time. A dusty clapboard affair, converted after the War, beside a hole-in-the-wall kebab & couscous joint. If we didn't manage to slip past the ticket lady we bought a concession pass for sixty pfennigs. Later we blagued the job of changing reels for the projectionist. That way we saw everything free from the windows of the projection booth.

The projectionist's name was Rolf, a Danziger who lived in a trailer-park. While we held the fort, Rolf would screw his girls on a mattress kept for that purpose backstage, behind the screen. Squinting, you could almost make out the silhouettes. The girls got a kick out of it & Rolf had them virtually lining up to take turns. Even if the mattress did stink of mildew & kerosene.

In the alleyway between the cinema & the couscous joint you could always smell fish heads baking in the sun where the cats dragged them from the garbage bins. But from the Arabs' kitchen, whose window opened right across from the projection booth door, there was the incomparable aroma of olive oil heating in a pan. Garlic. Cayenne pepper. Cardamom.

The projection booth was like an oven. That summer, the door was propped open every night & the tiny room flooded with cooking smells. There're certain films – *Querelle, Circle of Deceit, Escape Route to Marseille* – on which, for me, these olfactory sensations redolent of the Maghreb are indelibly imprinted.

One night a loud storm blew across the bay mid-screening. So loud you could barely hear the soundtrack. Someone came to the projection booth with a message: an eighteen-footer moored at the marina was beginning to drift. Rolf stopped the film – it was Lang's *Mabuse*, just when the silhouette tells the man & women how they won't leave the room alive – & made an announcement. Half the audience went out to help bring the

45

boat in. An interlude of high drama. Torch lights, voices across the water, the wailing of outboards beating against the wind. When everyone got back we rolled the film from where it'd stopped. The gunshots. The cardboard cut-out. The recorded voice.

In the evenings after leaving the cinema, we'd stay out at the marina or wander along the strand. We'd lie on a seawall & watch the constellations rise. All of space hung there like an eternity with boundaries. The watery horizon dipped & rose & shimmered as we looked up at the stars, searching for meteorites, imagining all the satellites up there orbiting. The MIR space station. The planets & moons & cosmic junk. The constellations & planets were all Roman. The moons, Greek. *Battle of the Titans* stuff. And further & further on, past the asteroid belts, a dark abyss punctuated by islands of light. Wolf always brought a deck of his mother's Lucky Strikes which we'd finish off before wheeling our bikes back across the fields. Guided by the mooring lights of the houseboats reflected on the black water of the inlet. The streetlights & the lights of the marina & the houses beyond that.

6
Bay of Angels

Hess stared down at the woman sitting on the opposite side of the table, the way someone stares who wants to attract a person's attention the better to disdain it. But the woman at the table failed to notice him. She sat reading, a dressmaker's mannequin in white linen blouse & beige slacks. Pale, thin, blonde, with fathomless eyes. Focused, so Hess couldn't help noticing, on a copy of *Le Figaro*.

The terrace of the Café San Vicenz was already filling for breakfast. Hess pulled out a yellow & red striped chair & sat down. A waiter appeared & Hess ordered a bottle of pastis. The waiter smirked. The blonde paid him no attention at all. *She thinks she can get the better of me*, he said to himself. Then aloud:

"Hell of a morning."

While the waiter sauntered off, Hess took in the other customers. Strange, he thought, how other people never seemed to possess any other function than of extras in a film. With no life but the one enacted on the surface of their expressions. Their inert presence. Exactly as if their appearances had all been arranged to form a backdrop to a scene. One in which a man, himself, had just approached a table on a seaside terrace & taken a seat opposite an attractive woman.

"Yeah, real hell of a morning."

The waiter reappeared with a bottle of Ricard & began arranging the table cloths on the tables nearby. Hovering. As Hess glanced at the breakfast menu a saccharine voice addressed a question at him from across the table. There was nothing on the menu that interested him.

"Late, almost midnight," he said in response. "Damn trains."

"You missed Louise?"

The woman who'd just spoken had a fragile complexion. Hess pictured her reddening in the sun. His gaze intentionally lingered over her body, her slim neck, her face in half-profile. She reminded him vaguely of Jeanne Moreau in *Baie des Anges*, only without the world-weariness. So probably not like Jeanne Moreau at all. Also the hair.

Her name was Adèle, & Luce had picked her up in Paris the year previous & taken her to Prague. Collected her, rather, like some exotic pet. Hess made a point of calling her Ada, because it irritated her. He mentally formed the two syllables, letting them sound there inside his head, one against the other, weakly. *Ah-dah*. Like a snake. Or the sound an infant makes before its learnt to say anything intelligible.

"Why, did she go somewhere?"

Ada's lips creased into a smile as she turned back to *Le Figaro*.

"That's to be seen," she replied.

Oh so enigmatically, Hess thought. Like the primadonna in a school play, who by herself conveys nothing of interest. He unstoppered the pastis & poured, setting the bottle back down with too much force. Then some water from a very tepid decanter. The combination turned a pale murky colour. Like fermented breast milk. "I don't have any definite plans," someone nearby was saying into their mobile phone. "From here on out," the voice said. "I got bored with what I was doing." Hess called to the waiter for some ice.

A cuntless neurotic, is how he'd summed Ada up after Luce first introduced them. Luce had pleaded for him to be civil, for her sake. Meaning she felt threatened? *Staking out her ground, more like.* He leaned back in his chair & eyed Ada across the table. Her face was turned in profile. He regarded the juxtaposition of the angles formed by the nose & lips. Her camera, he noticed, was lying on the chair beside her. She probably slept with it. He'd have to ask Luce when he saw her.

Just then the waiter returned with a tumbler of ice cubes. Also a basket of bread & croissants. Jam. Coffee. And a small jug of hot milk. Ada broke off a piece of crust then returned to her newspaper.

"Not tempted?"

He inflecting the bottle of pastis by way of a question mark.

"There's going to be another war," she said, not looking up.

Hess added ice to his drink, listening to the cracking sound the cubes made in the glass, then tasted it. The sun, which by now had climbed above the belfry, was hot in the sky though it wasn't yet nine o'clock. He thought: *When the bell sounds, it's to begin the killing?*

He said: "What's it this time?"

"South Lebanon," she answered. "Israel's invaded. It's because of those two conscripts who were kidnapped."

"You don't really believe that, do you?"

"It doesn't matter what I believe," she said, matter-of-fact.

Hess drained his glass. *Doesn't matter what I believe.* Where'd he heard that recently? He stared at his glass then down at the table. A wet ring marked the spot where the glass had sat & to which he now carefully returned it. *Of course, things exist whether we believe in them or not.* Wolf? Yes, Wolf. *Things exist.* It was trivial. The most trivial thing in the universe.

"You'll poison yourself," Ada said, turning the page.

She scanned it briefly before folding the newspaper & laying it on the edge of the table. *So what if I'm poisoning myself?* he thought. Faces stared up from a photograph cut in half, belonging to some calamity. BRUTALE ESCALADE AU PROCHE-ORIENT. Escalation in the Middle-East... Well, shit. Like any of that was news. At bottom right, a photo with a caption: «ENFANTS-BOMBES» AU DJIHAD. Kid suicide bombers. The photo was of an Iraqi boy, barely ten, in black military fatigues. Red & white headscarf & khaki vest packed with semtex. Semiautomatic in right hand. The very image of readiness. Anyone could see the kid a bright future.

Ada lifted the jug of hot milk in a very cautious, almost studied way, & poured the milk so it filled her coffee cup to the brim. He half hoped she'd spill it. *Serve her right.* But even as the thought formed itself he felt a headache begin to twitch again behind his eye. *There's no way to win. You're a drowning man & you've hardly even got your tongue wet!* He looked at his glass, anticipating a day spent in the onset of mindlessness & nausea. He poured another drink.

He'd awoken again, that morning, with a bleeding nose & a mouthful of blood, as if something had attacked him during the night. He remembered having fallen asleep just before dawn. And that he'd dreamt, but couldn't recall his dream. Everything was vague, shadows, with only a few bright spots. *Like Chinese lanterns on water*, he thought.

"You should probably eat something."

"I'm just working up an appetite," he said. "I was vaguely thinking of brochette. With lightly sautéed garlic & tomato. As soon as the sun rose above the belfry over there, I started thinking about tomatoes. Blood & tomatoes. It's curious, don't you think, how in certain languages – German, Spanish, English, French – the original name for that particular berry of the *Lycopersicon esculentum* has been preserved. Whereas in Italian they call it *pomodoro*. Like the apples of the Hesperides. While the ever-optimistic Slavs call it the fruit of paradise."

"Fascinating."

"The *Lycopersicon esculentum*," he continued, "is of the same family as Deadly Nightshade. One produces a prised fruit, the other a lethal poison. *Belladonna. Pomodoro.* Their very names, redolent of allegory. The fall of man, perhaps."

"Oh, the fall of man," she echoed, staring into her coffee.

"Such are the mighty inescapable themes. So now it's Lebanon's turn? Does *Figaro* draw a moral from the tale?"

But Hess had no interest in discussing the Middle East. The scenarios were always the same, inflected by the latest hysteria. Global pandemic of suicide bombings. Hijackings. Abductions. Sabotage. Katyusha missiles from the Gaza Strip, raining down on Haifa, Nahariya. Hearing Wolf go on about the eternal Intifada. Hess half-suspected Wolf's talk to be so much bullshit. That his real business was brokering funds, information, possibly even armaments. But Hess was a cynic, believing human beings, by & large, incapable of acting otherwise than opportunistically. Yet Wolf, he was forced to admit, was possibly that rare creature, both fanatic & opportunist. And this, Hess pondered, made him an infinitely more dangerous proposition.

"See for yourself," Ada broke in, nudging the paper towards him, disrupting the flow of his thoughts. And at that moment he remembered what his dream the previous night had been.

"You know," he said distractedly, "last night when I couldn't sleep, I kept thinking of this one time when Luce & I were stuck at the train station at Béziers. For hours. While they cleared a fire away from the tracks further down the line. I must've drifted off in the middle of it." He paused, refilling his glass. "Then I had a very strange dream. I don't normally remember my dreams. In fact I don't usually believe I dream at all."

"Must you?" Ada demanded, wearily, her eyes closed.

"Does it bother you?" Hess asked, again adding water & ice to his drink. "We were stuck at the same station," he continued before Ada could object. "Béziers. But instead of Luce, you were there. Isn't that funny? On one side of the tracks, beside the station house, there was a crowd of people with bags. Waiting. And on the other side of the tracks, their opposites. In every way identical only opposite. As though they were reflections in a very

52

large mirror. But not really reflections. They seemed alive, completely separate from the people they were supposed to be reflections of. There was something tragic about them, about their self-possession. The thing I remember most is you were standing beside me. You were desperately looking for yourself in the crowd on the other side of the tracks, without succeeding..."

"Why're you telling me this?"

"I thought it might interest you, seeing as you were in it."

"Other people's dreams never interest me. Besides, it's egotistical to expect other people to listen to your dreams."

"Oh, you know how it is. Easy to forget the world's not simply an amplification of my own aura."

He drank down the pastis, but the pastis was no longer satisfying. It tasted far too syrupy in his mouth. He wanted something bitter. Ada scrutinised him. Then in an abruptly different tone of voice, said:

"What would you say if I told you I'm going to have a child?"

"What I'd say?" Hess gave an aggressive laugh. "Why the hell are you asking me?"

"I'm serious."

"Have you told Luce?"

"No."

"Then I'd ask whether you intend to."

Instead of answering, she turned & gazed at the sea.

"Sometimes, I can't help myself, but when I look out there it seems like an empty mirror."

"Not so empty," Hess said.

"Perhaps what I mean is, I don't think Wolf's coming back."

Her expression was blank. Like something you'd spit in.

"Which's too bad," he said. "You think it's his, then?"

"Well there's no-one else, is there?"

"I don't see how I'm qualified to know that. Besides," he went on, "Wolf can't abide children. He's a fanatic. I assume you're keeping it?'"

"And what's that supposed to mean?"

Hess ignored her question. Her face twisted into contempt:

"Wolf said you were emotionally crippled. Now I know what he meant..."

"You don't know a damned thing about what he meant. Don't you realise? You're just a thing to him. Or *were*. To be made use of. A means to an end. Wolf doesn't believe in emotions. The emotions, my dear, aren't skilled labourers."

"You're full of shit, Hess."

"Fine. I'm full of shit. But you tell me, where's your precious Wolfie right now, this instant?"

Hess reached for the bottle while Ada glared at him. Silence now filled the space between them. He poured another drink. It was Ada who spoke first.

"He'll come back...," eyes glistening like wet stones.

"Sure, sure. Why wouldn't he come back?"

"There's something you're keeping from me, isn't there?"

Hess laughed.

"Look at me," he said, arms open wide in exaggerated pathos. "My life's a wreck. You want me to share my burdens with you?"

He let his arms drop. There was another long silence. Finally Ada spoke again.

"I don't know what Louise ever saw in you."

"You don't need to."

He looked away from her. Atop the belfry, a solitary seagull was perched on one leg. The clock read quarter past ten. A shout sounded in the street. Another rang out in answer from the beach. And all around on the terrace, the buzz of talk. The incidental music of chair legs scraping the ground. Spoons rattling against saucers. Steam venting from espresso machines.

7
rictis

The contrast between withdrawal
into one's self & otherness becomes
clearer when one compares man
with animals...
– José Ortega y Gasset

Man's tragedy, so Nietzsche says, is that he was once a child. Not because children are innocents who grow into monsters, common criminals, or mere failures. But because as we get older we lose our amorality & become enchained to the burden of right reason, duty, mission & sacrifice.

"Civilisation's based on the cockeyed notion that the father's dead & the mother's a virgin who experiences inexpressible pleasures." Which was Wolf's assessment, delivered one December morning at closing time outside a Prague nightclub, ten years ago. It'd been a long night & both of us were still disappointingly sober. "So you see," he said, "we're simply the logical consequence of a society that's finally begun to realise its own premises."

In the present it's 5:27 a.m. A heavy fatigue's come over me, but sleep's out of the question. I watch for the 7 to become 8 & think of Jean Renoir – *civilisation's just a sieve through which all the shit passes* – & realise for the last half-hour I've been sitting here staring at nothing. The blank space behind the photograph. The space between the lines written in the notebook. The corner of the room where the walls meet the ceiling like a vagina. Things slip in & out of awareness. Images, fragments of things, sending me off into these minor-key reveries. Till the inner screen goes

56

blank again. The signal drops out. Or I find myself awash in lines of static. Then switch channels. 5:35.

Three boys, just as they are in that photograph, their features, clothes, the scenery around them redolent of half-toned old East German cars. Three boys walking single file along a trail through sand dunes overgrown with spear grass as tall as they are. The grass casts rippling shadows across legs & torsos. It's morning, the sun still low in its arc, but already it's hot, only an intermittent breeze stirs the air. The three boys exit the dunes at a small clearing beneath a grove of pine trees. They immediately undress, draping their clothes & satchel bags from the lower branches of the trees. Then race each other down to the water. Though it's high tide, the water's still shallow & they have to wade far out to find somewhere to swim.

If you want to imagine what the world looks like upside down, you first have to believe you know what it looks like the right way around. It's a question of getting something into your grasp that's more than just air.

Rewind to the pine grove: three shirts hanging in the trees. I imagine myself standing there, in that clearing, searching through the branches for those figures wading across the estuary. I experience that dislocation encountered in dreams, when childhood scenes, memories, emotions intermingle with an adult awareness. It's tempting to look upon those discarded articles of clothing with a tragic eye, knowing what's to come. Like Wolf with his tragic view of history. But it isn't history that's tragic but how you go on experiencing it, dislocated within the self.

Our muted confessions, full of ellipses, were all we had to hold onto. As tenuous & incomprehensible to the outside world as walking through the sky. But to us, the stuff of unassailable truths. So when Wolf spat on the sand one day & said he wished his mother was dead, it didn't surprise us anymore than if he'd wished she was alive. Since in reality she hardly seemed to exist at all, like a TV spectre. Yet we envied Wolf. Perhaps we wished the same, in moments of futile, childish resentment. To resurrect the dead in order to see them buried, over & over again. If only so they couldn't abandon us.

Peering through the pine trees at the indifferent sky & mirroring sea, I catch sight of those former selves playing in the water. Leaping about. Careless. Unconcerned. And for all that unconcern, this scene communicates nothing more clearly than a sense of absence. I'm not there. I never was there. I'm merely this disconnected thing with memories that may as well belong to anyone. It'd make no difference if I'd invented them, since all they do is serve my present mood. A mood which compels me, though I contradict myself, to extract some sort of justification for my being stuck in this hotel room, waiting. What I mean is, I want to know why I've had to arrive at this particular time & place. Here & now. Because I can't escape the idea that even Ascher's suicide, perhaps his entire existence, was ultimately an instrument. Performing certain inescapable operations on this scenario I'm made to write & rewrite.

An Aryanised blonde with haunted, heavy-lidded eyes. Wolf's mother sometimes appeared on the beach, briefly, in the afternoons, wearing Italian sunglasses, to read a magazine on a deckchair while we lazed about keeping a wary eye on her. She popped tranquilisers like candy. Tyrosine, tryptophane, hyperforin, dextropropoxyphene. Like names in comic books. More often she stayed indoors watching reruns of *Landarzt* & other TV soaps she'd appeared in.

Wolf solemnly acted it out for us. How she'd park in front of the box in a dressing-gown, laughing to herself, late into the night. Till the test pattern came on. The image of that laughter disturbed & aroused us: the maternal spectre in black satin, face set in a mask of tense ambiguity, rocking back & forth. Her eyes. The shape of that mouth fixed in a kind of rictis.

Her resurrection after the rat poison in Wolf's story gave her an aura. She was the undead. A ghostly transmission from another world, pale & insubstantial as a starved vampire. She was Belladonna. The Black Widow. Medusa in sunglasses. In her we sensed that madness capable, in immaculately cold blood, of devouring its children.

Ascher's folks died in a car accident when he was ten. Their VW was hit by an express freight when the signal failed at a crossing outside Kiel. It was in the news. His older brother became his legal guardian & took over running the house. Ascher avoided him as much as possible. Ascher had a sister, too, but she moved out as soon as the brother made it known who was boss. He was a creep. The kind that can't help fucking with people.

Ascher had a pet rabbit that lived in a hutch made from an old shopping cart. We named it Frau Wenzel, after the fat lady who owned the concession at the marina under the old windmill. She wore this great white shapeless pinafore & knotted headscarf whose ends hung down over her shoulders like droopy rabbit ears. The hutch was at the back of Ascher's house, in view of the sand dunes, where no-one else went. He'd made a clearing in the spear grass, closed-off with scavenged palings & wire mesh. There were a couple of wicker beachchairs, *Strandkörbe*, with numbers painted on their sides & a striped umbrella. We'd congregate in the early afternoon & sit in the shade chewing gum

& reading comic strips or back issues of the cinema guides. We'd listen to music on a portable tape deck & dream up all kinds of idiotic schemes.

One day we were walking back from the beach across the field behind Ascher's place. As we approached the clearing, we noticed something hanging from a pole. It was the remains of Frau Wenzel. It'd been decapitated, then hung from a nail. A pool of clotted blood lay at the foot of the pole, swarming with ants & flies. The carcass, too, was covered with them. White fur smeared scarlet & black.

We expected Ascher to go off like a mad dog, but he said nothing. With a frightening calm he took the dead rabbit down off the pole & led us back across to the dunes to bury it. Wolf invented a ritual that involved pissing, so no dogs would come to dig the carcass up & eat it.

8

Bartók, Marlboro, Corniche

At just before nine a.m. the abandoned checkpoint at Cerbère flashed past. Without slowing, the white '76 model Triumph swerved onto the opposite side of the road, past a clutter of signage. *Bienvenido a España.* The woman in the green dress paid no attention, registering only the sound of the engine as it climbed & fell in a continuous rhythm. The coast flickered back into view as the road snaked around the Pyrenees foothills. Before she reached Port Bou, the sun rose over the water. She drove hard at it.

In Port Bou the traffic along the waterfront slowed almost to a crawl. A convoy of trucks passed in the opposite direction. She overtook recklessly. Then once more the road ascended steeply along the coast. At the next turn-off she swung the Triumph onto the motorway, re-crossing the border towards Rivesaltes. The engine wound to a crescendo. A dull continuous note & then a sudden explosion. Like a Bartók concerto.

The cross-border stretch of the A7 was virtually deserted. The speedometer fluttered above one-eighty, tarmac singing beneath the tyres. In a moment the singing became a howl. A sound like dogs hunting a wounded animal, & the road plunged beneath the mountains. A dull orange gloom stretching off to some invisible point. *All that matters*, she thought, *is to keep moving.*

Out of the tunnel the motorway scenery flashed back into view. Streaming under flyovers. Through open-cut channels feeding the southern arterials of the coastal cities. She drove at random, hair whipping about her face. Slowed & swung through the exit to Céret, heading inland perpendicular to the sea. Long stretches of straight, flat, poplar-lined road led across vineyard country. The mountains she'd just passed, arranged on her left in elaborate tiers. From Céret she followed the road to Canigou, its peak rising lopsided above the valley. At the cloister of St Martin's she stopped.

The silence was overwhelming. She sat in the car, head in hands. The cold air & stabbing sun worked their paradox upon her, till she felt in some way cleansed by it. A voice of weary disenchantment spoke within her. *On doit s'effacer complètement.* On doit. Complètement. *That's right*, she thought, *there's nothing left but to efface yourself completely. Begin again. As though you'd never existed before.* Existed. And then: *It's your fault. You should've waited for Hess. You should never've let Adèle go back to the room.*

The petrol station attendant gazed at the woman's bare feet as she crossed the driveway to the unlit shop. Then shifted his gaze to the car she'd just gotten out of, as if attempting to solve an unexpected problem. He was standing in the garage entrance, both hands in the pockets of blue overalls, chewing something. When the woman had almost reached the shop door he picked the thing he'd been chewing out of his mouth & cleared his throat. The woman, who hadn't seen him at first, backed up & regarded him silently. He nodded.

"What'll it be?"

"I'm out of cigarettes."

He gestured in the direction of a vending machine, wedged between crates of oil & brake fluid: "Right behind ya." After a moment he added: "Want me t' fill 'er up?"

The woman glanced around at the vending machine. "I don't have change," she said simply.

"'s okay. What's she take? Leaded I s'pose. Bit of a guzzler, eh? Reckon she must have a fair few miles on 'er by now. Good nick tho'. Don't get many a them pommy jobs up 'ere. Nice."

Up here, she repeated to herself. Supposing he must've meant altitude, rather than latitude. She scanned the brand names on the front of the machine, presumably meant to correspond to what was inside.

"Don't you have Gauloise?"

"See that sign," the attendant pointed without her seeing him. Beside the shop door there was a metal sandwich board with a red & white triangular design. And below it in black lettering, the word MARLBORO. "Can only stock those. That's what the company pays for. Free market that's called."

"You mean," Louise said, looking past the attendants' left shoulder, "I don't have a choice?" She thought: *Things happen. There's no way of knowing why.*

"Well, it's like this," he grinned idiotically. "Choice is regular or lights."

"Regular or lights?"

"Yeah. Simpler that way, don't ya reckon?"

She paused to consider this for a moment.

"Regular then."

She thought: *Reasons are only put in your way to confuse you?*

The attendant stared at her for a while longer, then went across & opened up the machine, pulling out a large red & white carton.

"Don't work, nohow. Just what's used for storage. Y'only want one? Cos there's plenty more in 'ere."

He straightened up & handed her the packet he'd extracted from the carton, looking at her more quizzically now.

"You'll be wantin' me t' fill 'er up, then?"

She took the cigarettes & glanced around as if searching for something. The attendant anticipated her:

"Ladies room's out back."

She nodded slowly, as if considering the meaning of his words. She began walking in the direction the attendant had indicated. He called after her:

"So I'll just fill 'er up then, okay?"

The bathroom was really just a cubicle with a washbasin, paper towels & a mirror. A hole in the ground against the back wall gave off a thick stench of ammonia. As soon as she looked in the mirror, she saw why the attendant had been staring at her the whole time. Her face was an utter mess. She doused some paper towels & wiped away the ruined mascara & lipstick as best she could. Then wiped herself beneath her dress, tossing the soiled paper into the hole. Then she unwrapped the cellophane from the pack of Marlboros.

While the attendant was busy with the Triumph, she walked down to the end of the driveway & lit a cigarette. There were pine trees all along the road & up the sides of the valley. Some houses back along the road suggested there'd once been a village thereabouts, but she hadn't seen any signs.

As she smoked her cigarette, a tractor drove past. A pair of eyes stared out at her from the cabin. She thought: *At least you didn't see their faces. So you'll never have to see them again.* She could hear the petrol pump droning in the background. *But what if they recognise you? What if they think you're some kind of slut who likes it? What if they do it again?* The driveway was cold beneath her feet.

"She's all set," the attendant called out. "Nothin' else?"

The woman didn't answer. After she'd stubbed-out her cigarette, she found the attendant sitting behind the cash register in the shop, picking his teeth. He watched her come in & nodded.

"Everything okay?"

"How much?" she asked.

"An even forty, sweetheart," he said.

She unfolded two notes & laid them on the counter. He

gazed after her as she walked back to the Triumph, pushing his tongue against the back of his teeth. A low hissing sound emanating from his mouth.

The woman in the green dress slowed the Triumph at the turnoff to Collioure, following the road to her right as it wound across the hillside. She paused to take in the view across the corniche. The sea & the shimmer of hot air over it. The sea looked swollen & agitated at the same time. Like a thick stew about to boil. Swollen. Agitated. The air stank of sour wine.

Pulling back onto the road she had to swerve to avoid the carcass of a brown dog, virtually sheered in half across the lane markers. Her head swam. For a second she saw herself sitting there at the steering wheel screaming, hysterical, like someone in a movie. *The Woman in the Green Dress.* She stamped the accelerator to the floor & the image flashed, was gone. Only the sound of the tyres. Her breathing. Her heartbeat.

By luck, she found a parking space right in front of the boulangerie, beside the little hotel she'd been staying in since the end of May. Madame Fournier, the hotel's proprietress, was deep in conversation with the boulanger's wife. The sun was already above the rooftops & a heavy shadow, cast by a striped awning across Madame Fournier's face, almost blotted her out.

"Bonjour!" Madame Fournier called. And immediately resumed her dialogue with her well-fed neighbour.

One hand shading her eyes, the woman in the green dress searched the upper floor of the hotel for a sign. The shutters on Hess's balcony were open, but he wasn't to be seen. She remained standing by the car, unsure how to proceed, each observed detail interposing between her & the possibility of deciding what to do. Finally, too self-conscious to stay where she was, she crossed the street & stepped inside the hotel.

After groping in the gloom for her key behind the reception desk, she crept up the stairs as quietly as she could. She needn't've been concerned. Hess's door was wide open & the maid was cleaning his room. Evidently he was somewhere in the village. She unlocked the door of her own room & slipped in unobserved. *If Hess comes up...* she thought. But it didn't complete. She tried to recall what her argument with Adèle had been. But she couldn't remember anything. She couldn't even remember how she'd driven to Canigou. Everything was a blur. *Life*, she thought, *is improvised in the teeth of catastrophe.* Her life, her own catastrophe? Or something else? The human catastrophe. Catastrophe on a cosmic scale. The lesser for the greater...

Though the room was hot, she was shivering. She sat on the edge of her bed. Sunlight through shuttered windows caught the dust motes hanging in the air. She was still wearing the emerald green dress she'd gone out dancing in the night before. One of the seams had torn. It all felt so long ago. They'd been waiting for Hess to arrive & then something happened. Adèle had gone off in a huff back to the hotel, leaving her alone. She remembered the lights in the square. The music. The crowd. The weightlessness. But Hess hadn't come. And then she'd got lost. And she was still lost, not knowing what to do.

She let her handbag & keys fall to the floor. Slumped down onto the bed, eyes fixed on the light fixture in the middle of the ceiling. Then, in a mechanical reflex, she dragged upright & crossed to the bathroom. Retched into the sink. A grey mask hung in the mirror. In her mind the embryo of a thought was unconsciously forming. Without discernible shape & without words. Behind the mirror, among the litter of toiletries, she found a bottle of progestin past its expiry date & emptied the pills into her hand. They seemed too small to undo anything.

9
shot-for-shot

Cinematography is, first & foremost,
montage.

– Sergei Eisenstein

You want to bore the shit out of yourself, go ahead, just don't involve me in your plans. The proverbial crack in the wall. Waiting for a flicker of light from the other side. The bright idea. Well someone has to have it.

Begin with a twitch in the eye, a nervous tick at the back of the mind. Make a technology out of that. Some *Wizard of Oz* gadget to set everything into a constant agitation, confuse the issue, upset the applecart. Something which has no other consequence than to fool the eye, make a shimmering Xanadu of nothing. A dream, a fragmented action. It moves & talks! In place of something you're not permitted to see.

They have a name for that. Only now they park you in front of a TV instead of freighting you off to the nuthouse. You get your hallucinations sanctioned from on-high. Pre-packaged mindwash. Guaranteed to numb the cortex, relieve whatever ails, put the snore on you. A pipe dream on three valium a day, coursed by time-lapse shadows.. A swarming singular image going nowhere. A test-patterned Rorschach blot.

The migraine's steadily getting worse. I grope around in my travel bag for painkillers & finally succeed in locating some

Ibuprofen. I take four, not caring what effect the combination with Nembutal might produce. My liver's probably fucked anyway. Lucky there's no mini-bar in the hotel room. I know booze would only make things worse, but I can't always help myself. It's just another one of the problems I haven't managed to take control of. Booze & mediocrity.

When did the migraines begin? I don't know. It was after I jumped ship & left the sacred Fatherland behind. The migraines came with the writing, the sleeplessness, drinking in the middle of the night, not eating, slowly breaking myself, all to no avail. Perhaps I'll feel better later on, tomorrow, the next day, when it's all over. The sort of crap I tell myself so I don't have to face facts. I decide to lie down again, or else my body decides for me. Just a few minutes till I regain my equilibrium. As I shut my eyes there's a picture of a man in a white suit, standing at the end of the Laboe marina, watching me. I don't know who he is. He seems vaguely familiar. Rectangular black-rimmed glasses, slightly balding. I wait for something to happen but nothing does. Privately I call him the Continuity Man.

Then everything goes black. For a moment I enter a dream. It's a dream of a sleep in which there's no longer any recurring scene about the marina, or the beach where I used to play as a child, or Ascher or Wolf, or anybody. It's a black sleep in which I dream of blackness. And then I fall out of the bed & it's white. I'm completely surrounded by it & then I see I'm awake. In those few brief moments I must've entirely separated from my body. I look at my hands propping me up from the floor & realise I'm shaking. Coming from somewhere deep within. Like a switch being repeatedly flicked. I'm numb all down my side, but the migraine isn't there anymore. Or I feel it, but it's no longer present, not in the way it was just a minute ago.

It takes a lot of effort just to concentrate on getting up. Finally I make the bathroom. The bed's in disarray, as though evidence of some sort of struggle. I look at myself, at my body, still lying there on the bed, staring at my projected image: the one staggering across the room who turns & is consciously aware of all this while it's happening. Perhaps I'm that man in the dream, too. My suit jacket lies crumpled at the foot of the bed. Fading to white. Do I expect the jacket to sit up by itself, a headless ghost, & begin addressing me, like an alter ego? And what would it say? *You're a fraud! You're fictionalising yourself, your past, you may as well say you came from the moon.* But I was never any good at that. Perhaps it'd just point at me, the man without substance, & say: *You treat life as if you were remaking someone else's film.*

No. *Exactly* remaking someone else's film, *shot-for-shot.* Knowing that everything I've ever made up my mind about shakes apart, has already shaken apart, & I'm not able to put the pieces back together, because I don't understand them. They're pieces of an *alien* life, a *completely* alien life. Like being locked in an editing room with a pile of random out-cuts I'm supposed to splice together into sequence. To establish some sort of continuity by any means possible. With the added constraint that I'm only allowed to see each of the frames once.

Even an idiot knows there's no going back. The past, like a dream, forever slipping away, a film running backwards faster than the mind can grasp it. But still you want to freeze the frame, the face, the gesture, the place. The exact place, for example, among the boulders at the end of the beach where the three of us used to perv on the topless sunbathing women. I tell myself it exists, this place. That it exists *in reality.* That it isn't just in my head. As if, stepping away from the film, I could still choose to enter the scene, out there in the world: a beach, pine trees, an outcrop. Things that can be objectively described, with all the clarity of light filtered through water. Whose distortions render everything in greater immediacy. The silvered rippling of a mirror come alive. Air that's molten glass. Viscous. A tangible substance.

I see myself, standing there at the end of the path between the dunes, perceiving it all. The scene, the figures in it. But this doesn't mean a thing. I'm as far off as it's possible to be. A distorted memory. The ghost of a memory. A phantom limb that aches in the night when you try to sleep.

10
Morte aux Tièdes!

There'll be no hope for man till he returns to the caves.

It was just before Wolf left for the Middle East. Something in his words conveying a purity of purpose only lunatics ever attain. Returning to first principles. It brought to Hess's mind a fearful cringing in the night. Fugitives. Men, women. Huddled in view of a sky torn by lightning-flash. Thunder. Snarling copulations in the gloom. Later, perhaps, there'd be campfires with ape-men huddling around, fending off the cold. Apprehensive of the shapes that loomed from cave walls like angry spirits, demanding sacrifice. The dance of shadows, fire, thunder, lightning-flash. Voices of God. Primeval cinema, fixating the neolithic mind. Evolving it.

When he thought of Wolf, everything was black-&-white. Grey. All shades closing in. Blotting everything else out. Man & the fanaticism of his own existence. Man on his path to godhead. Slouching through landscapes resistant to metaphor, radiantly blank. Was it a road necessarily to be endured, running back towards whatever he himself was escaping? Had his own life, his individual actions, ever so much as amounted to something? Something yet to be discovered?

Hess sat watching the people on the beach. So much dross & flotsam. The beguiling calm of the sheltered sea. And the sky, that particular sky, like a canvas on which Time cast itself in bold figurations. Suggestively incomplete. He was on his third glass of pastis.

"Tell me about him," Ada said.

"Who?"

"You know who."

"There's nothing to say."

"Tell me anyway."

"We knew each other, that's all."

"I mean before."

"We were children."

What else, he thought, *was there to say?* The truth, he knew, would only be unpleasant. Ada's voice drifting across the gap between them, somehow unreal. Hess continued to stare at the horizon. His own voice seemed to come out of nowhere.

"What're you thinking?" she asked.

"I'm thinking how the human condition's like an audience whose members are always surprised when they're required to become actors."

Someone else's words in his mouth. *Your problem*, he recalled Wolf telling him, *is you're too far up your own arse*. They'd been drinking in a bar. Wolf had just returned from Cuba. *Everything's just ideas to you. Words. You can't get a grasp of their reality. Everything's always flat, two-dimensional. It's time you learned to see things from an historical perspective*. But why shouldn't truth to like something you could just go out & find lying on the street? Who the fuck needed an historical perspective, when the world's right in front of your face? Yet that was exactly what Hess had always been afraid of, because he knew the truth had never existed for him like that. Everything life had taught him made him believed in the need to inhabit the gap between words & silence. To pass through error into the night of creation. The inner night.

Wolf's insistence on belief-at-all-costs stemmed from his disappointment at having grown up at the fag-end of a defeated ideology. Glasnost. Perestroika. When the Wall came down, History itself had been abolished. NO FUTURE writ large on the cosmic TV. The world-as-we-knew-it went through the motions of adjusting the picture. Waving placards against the neo-fascists, the World Bank, the IMF, the Gulf War, wasn't enough. The protests were empty, conscience-soothing. Like sorbet. The only thing that changed was the illusions got reconciled.

After Bosnia, Wolf joined a succession of more & more radical groups. He was looking for the edge. A simple & at the same time complicated violence grew within him. The hunger of a violence seeking itself. To meet head-on in the cataclysm of some vast overturning. And if not the promised Revolution, any destruction of complacencies would do. *Morte aux tièdes!* Death to the lukewarm, to the domesticated, to the middle-way & to the middle-classes. In the mouth of anyone else, it might've sounded ridiculous. And so Hess had laughed. Halfheartedly, cynically, uneasily, dubiously. *Tiède*. Unable to guess the depth of Wolf's fanaticism.

It was this fanaticism that seduced Ada. She'd clung to him, for an instant, & now he was gone again. Like a character in a novel, she made gestures at deserving her existence. But only gestures. A preview of coming attractions. Anything more was beyond her grasp. After a long silence & without conviction, Hess asked:

"What'll you do?"

Simply because it was what his character in this drama was expected to ask & he vaguely felt pity for her. His voice seemed to startle her. Hess watched her struggling, fascinated with the effect his words produced. He thought: *It doesn't matter anyway. Does it?* Then: *She's like something that's out of mind as soon as you turn a corner.*

"I don't know," she shook her head at last.

Of course you don't, he thought. *It passes. These things always do.* But she, of course, understood the question differently. And what she understood couldn't be passed off. The facts required her to make a decision. To act, like Medea, tempting herself towards one or another form of damnation.

Below the terrace, the shadows were in retreat & a hot breeze settled beneath the umbrellas, stirring them in their moorings. The little flags atop the masts in the harbour fluttered, then fell slack. Fell slack & then fluttered. Soon the full heat of the day would be upon them. Fire raging in the sky. The sea aflame. And couched on their beds of stone, the damned, prostrate in ritual pain & ecstasy.

All of a sudden Ada turned towards him, tears in her eyes. Like Maria Falconetti in Dreyer's *Jean d'Arc*. That silent terror in the exchange of looks, shot-reverse-shot, between Falconetti & the mad monk Artaud. Woman & man. Martyr & prelate. History's revenants, like blackened celluloid dolls. And right before his eyes she began to dissolve, a piece of film erupting into invisible flame. And he wanted to tell her they were all equally damned, no matter what their crimes.

But she wasn't there, where she'd been before, across the table. He was alone. The bottle empty. *Just a moment ago a man & woman were sitting here. For a moment, this table was the centre of their universe.* He waited, he didn't know why, for her to reappear. *Perhaps,* he thought, *inside the film we're all dreaming, it's really the film that dreams us?* Dry mouthed. Eyes burning. He stared into the light, thinking of the old men playing pétanque along the canal, till the waiter came & cleared the props away.

11

urban guerrilla concept

> They'll kill us all. You know what
> kind of pigs we're up against. This's
> the Auschwitz generation. You can't
> argue with people who made
> Auschwitz.
>
> – Gudrun Ensslin

Death fascinated Wolf, even as a child. Radicals from the 70s, like the Red Army Faction, obsessed him. He kept a scrap book with old newspaper clippings & all sorts of things. Mogadishu. The Baader-Meinhof suicide prison photos. And he owned a copy of Meinhof's *Urban Guerrilla Concept*, red star & Heckler-&-Koch on the front cover, scrounged from a junkshop: *The RAF intends to temporarily put specific parts of the State's government & security apparatus out of action. This will destroy the myth of the overwhelming nature & invincibility of the System…*

Wolf was always plotting some sort of make-believe insurgency. He had an entire programme worked out, patched together from scraps of Mao & Ho Chi Minh, which he'd spout from his proverbial soapbox while we lounged about on Ascher's beachchairs egging him on, a central committee of three. Like good little revolutionaries we inflated ourselves with a righteous sense of urgency & singularity of vision. Instead of parables & proverbs we fired ourselves up with slogans, proscriptions, all sorts of dialectical nonsense.

We parroted: *No region of the world can today achieve the transition to stability & democracy through peaceful means. The crisis is lurching towards its climax. To be cut off in parochialism or to postpone the struggle means being caught up in a vicious circle of ever-worsening decline...* What crisis? Which struggle? It didn't matter. Any crisis would do. The struggle was all. Struggle for the sake of struggle!

During our periodical raids on the boatsheds near the marina, Wolf found a rusty bayonet from a Mauser-98 carbine, some cardboard shooting targets & a brown leather shoulder-holster discoloured by sweat & hardened by the salt air. There were boxes of shell casings & an old starter's gun. We stashed everything behind Ascher's house, under a trapdoor hidden by tall grass. The cell's secret cache. There were jars of potassium & ammonium nitrate, & coils of magnesium Wolf planned to use for a bomb, to blow up the US naval base at Kiel.

Wolf's brilliant idea was to stage a bank robbery to raise cash, the way they did in films. *Bonny & Clyde*. We all pitched in. It was an elaborate business. As a political concept, bank robbery, like hostage-taking & hijacking, needed a certain amount of finesse. We pitted criminality against necessity & argued capitalist greed (it was the eighties). As usual, Wolf arbitrated by quoting the beloved Meinhof: *Legality*, he sang out, *is about power. The position of legality in relation to illegality is determined by the contradiction between reformist & fascist tendencies in government...*

But to pull a bank job we figured you needed weapons & to get weapons you needed money. It was a vicious circle no amount of dialectics could break. As a stopgap we improvised, built an arsenal out of the near-at-hand. After all, you didn't need someone's safety deposit box to make a bomb from pigshit & fertiliser. A manifesto appeared on Ascher's toolshed wall:

Legality, it said, *is the ideology of parliamentarianism, the social partnership, the plural society. Many of those attempting to challenge the system ignore the fact that telephones are being legally bugged. That the post's being scrutinised. That neighbours are being legally questioned. That informers are being paid. And that all this State activity's legal. The organisation of political work & activism — if you want to keep away from the eyes of State scrutiny – has to take place on an illegal level, as well as the legal one…*

We refuse to rely on some spontaneous anti-fascist mobilisation in the face of this kind of State terror…

To be an urban guerrilla means to launch an offensive against imperialism. The Red Army Faction is striking the connection between the legal & illegal resistance. Between national & international resistance. Between national & international struggle…

The Urban Guerrilla Concept means that, despite the weakness of revolutionary forces in the Federal Republic & West Berlin, we intend to make a revolutionary intervention: HERE & NOW!

Our cell was supposed to have a name & insignia, which Ascher designed, & uniforms. He drew page after page of these sinister Harlequins, like mad Picassos with submachine guns. We'd just seen Fassbinder's *Third Generation* the week before & Ascher decided we should wage class war dressed like Hana Schygulla, with clown wigs & face paint. No-one, he said, would ever suspect us. Besides, clowns did crazy stuff all the time. People'd think it was some kind of gag. Wolf contributed a defiant-sounding slogan borrowed from one of his pamphlets: AMNESTY EQUALS PACIFICATION. Whatever the hell that was supposed to mean.

The idea was hot for about a month before it ran out of steam & got put on ice. On TV one night there was a newsflash about a Vietnam vet strafing a prefab burger joint with an M16, in Poughkeepsie, NJ. The presenters didn't say anything about politics or multinational corporate conspiracy. They just said the vet was deranged.

The highpoint of our terrorist careers came when we pulled off one of those idiotic stunts only a kid would be dumb enough to dream up. It centred on an old-timer who lived alone in a cottage on a plot of land abutting the north end of the beach. His name was Joost & he stammered. Even in summer he wore a cloth cap, long-sleeved shirts with the cuffs buttoned & collar turned up, & trousers, with canvas tennis shoes that'd once been white but had long since turned a pale green. On account of his spending half of every day keeping his lawn down with a clanking push mower. My auntie said he'd been a stevedore during the War, having been unfit for military service. Autistic, she said.

We'd regularly see Old Joost carting buckets of cut flowers to Frau Wenzel. Chrysanthemums, carnations, tulips. Frau Wenzel displayed them in her concession, on a counter beside jars of candy, eucalyptus, liquorice & chocolate drops. The flowers never smelt of anything, except fertiliser. They grew in three squat glasshouses at the back of Joost's cottage. There were fruit & nut trees along one side which somehow defied the salt air & thin soil. And rose bushes, too, weirdly out of place. A field of yellow-flowered rape adjoined the eastern side of his plot & stretched across to a channel with embankments that ran in a straight line to the sea.

Wolf proposed we sneak into Old Joost's cottage & see what was inside. Willing to believe just about anything for a lark, it didn't take much to convince us the old man was hiding a sinister past. We settled on the theory that Joost had been assistant gimp to some concentration camp psychopath like Mengele. Playing the Marty Feldman character to Gene Wilder's Frankenstein. The fiendish Doktor had conducted experiments in Auschwitz, using Jews & Siamese twins to manufacture a zombie doomsday race. Test-tube *Untermenschen*. Slaves to the Doktor's mind-control, programmed to rise up from the crematoria like golems to destroy the enemies of the Reich. But when the Yanks captured Auschwitz, the quack Doktor slipped

82

the cordon with pockets full of gold teeth, headed to South America. Doktor Fausto, he called himself. He was still alive & kicking four years before our little plot was hatched. 1979. They never caught him. Drowned in the Atlantic. It didn't hit the news till '85, when they dug up his grave & figured who he really was.

But it was no secret most of the Nazis had stayed put, simply swapped their armbands for veterans' benefits. Twentyfive years after the War, the GDR was *still* being run by a gang of war criminals, evil masterminds straight out of a Marvel comic strip. Federal Judges, Leaders of State Assemblies, Ministers & Secretaries of State, Heads of the Confederation of Industry, Federal Chancellors. No fewer than three of the six Presidents of the Federal Republic, all ex-NDSAP & SS. Proof, if proof was needed, of conspiracy on a vast scale. Everywhere you looked, there they were. GSG9, CIA, Stasi, KGB, Mossad even. It was enough to make you puke.

"They don't waste talent like that," Frau Wenzel tutted, pointing out something in the newspaper about a chief engineer at I.G. Farben.

It wasn't the sort of thing they taught in school. Everything we knew about the Nazis came from movies. *Salon Kitty, Die Verdammten, The Serpent's Egg, The Night Porter.* Mid-winter, when Laboe was a ghosttown, Rolf would sit all night in the projection booth rolling joints, digging through suitcases of whatever reels were doing the rounds & run through them till he found something that took his fancy. Dubbed kitchen sink, psychedelic, hard-boil. Anything at all. These would turn into private screening for whichever out-of-town chick he was balling at the time. He'd leave us to keep an eye on the reels & retire backstage with crosseyed Helga or Mausi or Christina with the big arse. Rolf didn't give a toss about politics.

Once he got started, Wolf could spout agitprop non-stop. Something about the fervour of it shot us full of pure adrenaline.

The maniac kill-all-the-fuckers look on his face whenever he denounced The System.

The System: a cosmic neo-Nazi plot to enslave humanity, transmitting its malevolent designs through TV & mass psychology fascist consumerism. Cue Bela Lugosi with swastika & doomsday box. We swore death to fascists & bawled slogans. *A clear dividing line*, we decided, *must be drawn between ourselves & the enemy!* The nuclear family. Christian Democrats. Pigs in suits. Wolf laid out the plan. We'd unmask the conspiracy from the ground up. Out the collaborators. Expose the filth among us.

Joost the gardener was a simp. The ideal kind of mindwash proxy to stooge for The System. Wolf made the call. We'd ransack the old man's cottage for evidence, then mete out justice. At dusk, the three of us in our regimental clown suits, snuck through the pine grove at the back of Joost's cottage. Wolf with bayonet stuffed into his shorts, Ascher with his starter's gun. In the warm evening air, the smell of pine needles mingled with the faint distant scent of the estuary & the smell of canola & cut grass. We waited till dark, then crept up between the fruit trees. Three grim little clowns stalking the shadows.

The sound of crickets died off as we advanced, signalling our approach. In the cottage, nothing stirred. Headlights swept across the fields illuminating the glasshouses. We skirted the back of the cottage & took up positions on the side furthest from the road. The bathroom window had been left half-open. Ascher boosted Wolf up so that he could climb in. It was a heavy wood-framed sash window, the sort that slide up. As soon as Wolf began squeezing through, he dislodged a piece of curtain rod that was keeping it propped open. With a thunk the window clamped down on the his shorts, backside sticking out & legs, bug-like, writhing in the air.

The more we pushed, the worse it got. Wolf's shorts snagged on the window latch while the rest of him slid headfirst into Joost-the-gardener's toilet. There was a loud clatter & the sound of flushing water. We looked up to see Wolf's feet gone but his torn shorts still dangling from the sill. A moment later the back door of the cottage opened & there stood a snarling, sodden, bare-arsed clown wielding an antique bayonet. It couldn't've been a more auspicious beginning.

The cottage was pitch dark inside with a stink of kerosene. We stumbled around till our eyes adjusted. Wolf led the way through the interior gloom, stalking on tiptoes. There was nothing to hear except an old wall clock ticking & our breathing. Precisely ordered junk littered every available space. We crept around with no set purpose, running into things & each other at regular intervals. Wolf riffled through the junk, looking for proof of the great conspiracy. Then we froze. We'd wandered into a room with no windows. Something damp brushed against my hand, or else my hand brushed against it. Ascher felt it too.

Then it moved, groaned. Wolf shouted RUN! & Ascher's gun went off with a deafening clap. We careened pell-mell through the labyrinth trying to find a way out, pursued by a crazed cannibal. The back door flew open & three little clowns tumbled down the steps, face first in a patch of freshly turned manure, a tangle of arms & legs. A light went on inside & we fled, holding onto our clown wigs, Wolf's bare white arse leading the way. Behind us, the sound of breaking glass rang out through the night. The starter's gun had landed on one of the glasshouse roofs, flung from Ascher's hand in panic as we sprinted towards the cover of the pine trees, high on each other's fear.

12
White Porcelain

Luce didn't look at him when he came into the room. Head tilted back, eyes fixed on the fan turning slowly overhead. She was sitting on the bed in a patterned bathrobe, back against the bed-head, legs straight out. The bedspread was coarse, maroon & white stripes. She looked like someone in an advertisement for something. Domestic Bliss Incorporated.

"Hello stranger," Hess grinned.

He sat sideways on the edge of the bed. Luce continued staring at the fan. He'd found the Triumph parked on the street outside. It seemed as good a reason as any to come up.

"Am I intruding on something?"

Luce shook her head, still not looking at him. He reached out & traced a line along one of her shins, encircling her ankle with the fingers of his left hand. Her skin was cool & smelled of soap. He couldn't feel her pulse. A pair of flies were hovering in the middle of the room. On the writing desk, a pile of notes teetered under a glass ashtray full of cigarette butts. A catalogue was lying open on the floor, a colour reproduction of a painting spread across both pages. *Le Faubourg de Collioure*, 1905. Fishing boats with red masts on a beach, black hills rising in the background.

"Been busy, eh?"

On the nightstand a poorly extinguished cigarette butt lay smouldering in a second ashtray, this one made of white porcelain. He leant forward to snuff it out completely, pausing as he did so to smell Luce's hair. It made him think of a scene from a film, with a woman lying on a bed, naked beneath a sheet, bare shouldered. Still young, still beautiful.

Maybe it wasn't a film. Maybe it was just a memory. Paris. In the semi-darkness of a room, a voice, the sound of rain. *Not lies*, the voice said, *only obstacles*. The silhouette of someone, him, bent-over a reclining woman. The suggestion of a kiss. Lips, tongue, teeth. Implied, not seen. After, lying there, motionless, side-by-side. The scent of the woman's hair...

"Luce?"

The inertia of her. As if waiting for the heat to let up. Or the flies in the middle of the room to drop dead. Or the slough of some former self. A freshly washed corpse in a bathrobe. Everything that'd just gone through his head, he realised, was the opposite of the reality in that room. Sitting on the edge of his wife's bed. Evocations of morbidity. Half expecting to look down & sees flies crawling across her face. His face was hot, flushed. The room was stifling. He didn't know how she could bear to lie there so still.

"I'm drunk," he said. "And I've got a headache. I'm going for a swim. To cool down. Been nice talking to you..."

"Hess," she interrupted him, gesturing towards a packet of cigarettes just out of reach on the bedside table. Marlboro. In the process, her fingertips brushed a box of matches & it fell to the floor. "Be a darling."

Hess regarded her for a moment before bending down & picking it up. He tapped a cigarette out of the packet & lit it, then handed it to his wife.

"I didn't think you liked Marlboro."

"It's all they had."

She blew a long stream of smoke at the ceiling. Hess watched it coil & eddy & gradually disperse.

"We must've just missed each other," he said. "Got in after midnight. Found your note at reception. I went to look for you but got sidetracked somehow. You know how it is."

He paused. She said nothing.

"Damn trains."

Luce still said nothing.

"You're not angry at me are you?"

"No. How was your trip?"

"Terrible."

Luce drew on the cigarette. Her hand shook. There were now three flies hovering beneath the fan. Hess watched Luce watching them. He couldn't decide whether to stay or leave.

"Guess who I ran into just now?" he said. "Only dear Adèle." He regarded her quizzically. "Now isn't that a nice coincidence? As a matter of fact we've just been having breakfast together, like a couple of old bed fellows."

He paused again. No reaction.

"Which we almost are, wouldn't you say? Only no-one would've guessed it from our conversation. Seems she doesn't approve of me." He tapped her shin bone with his index finger but her eyes remained fixed. "You know, Luce, life's too fucking short for this carry-on."

He attempted a laugh, but it came out like the sound of somebody being choked.

"You know what she's like," Luce said, shifting the weight of her head to one side.

"No, what's she like?"

"Demanding. I feel watched."

Her face sagged slightly as she spoke, becoming older.

"It was your idea." He glanced at the column of ash lengthening at the end of her cigarette.

"Maybe it's just the work," closing her eyes. "I can't seem to breathe, it's… smothering me. The whole thing was a mistake."

"Luce, if there's anything…"

"Yes?"

The ash fell onto the bathrobe without her noticing. She seemed already to've forgotten about the cigarette. Hess inspected his fingernails.

"Anyway, it's not Adèle. It's me. I'm… I'm probably just…"

Hess yawned, becoming bored with the conversation.

"D'you remember Wolf?" he asked.

"How could I forget the man I spent my wedding night with?" she said, holding the remainder of the cigarette out to him. "Here, get rid of that for me, will you?"

It was true. Wolf had been one of the witnesses at the civil ceremony. The three of them had got completely drunk afterwards & fell asleep in the same bed in a Prague hotel. He couldn't remember who the other witness was. He took the butt from her & stubbed it out in the already overflowing ashtray.

"He turned up while you were in Paris. I didn't tell you. He was seeing Ada."

"They know each other?"

Luce looked at him for the first time since he'd come in.

"Not really," Hess said. "Let's just say she reminds him of his mother. *On revient toujours à ses premiers amours.* You know, when we were kids…"

"Don't tell me," she interrupted. "You shared your little Oedipal fantasies with each other…"

Hess waved her away.

"Oh, I forgot. You didn't have a mother. Well, I'm sure you compensated."

"Luce," Hess shook his head.

"So, Wolfie's been sniffing about the henhouse? I thought he was busy fighting injustice."

"There was that, too. We argued about politics."

"You always do. It's a sign of impotence, Hess. All that talk about revolution's just exhausted libido. I've always had the impression he's angry at you for not being in love with him."

"Jesus, Luce," Hess responded, suddenly feeling depressed. "Anyway, he left about a week ago. For Beirut. All very sudden.

One day he's back from Cuba, head full of Castro's latest epic bullshit, raving about Chavez & the whole Bolivarian circus act. The next he's off to run guns for the Jihadis. Right in the thick of it. They're always blowing each other up over there for no good reason."

"There're good reasons for people blowing each other up?"

Luce was looking at the flies again. She ran a finger beneath her left eye & along the bridge of nose. The fan seemed to be doing nothing but shift hot air around. The curtain in the doorway to the balcony hadn't moved the entire time. It struck Hess as symptomatic that Wolf should have developed a fascination with the very people who'd killed his own father. He let the thought pass. His hand, he realised, had gone back to holding Luce's ankle. Her ankle was cold & now so were his fingers.

"By the way," he said, massaging his hand. It felt strange to his touch. Somehow alien, dead. Gradually the feeling returned in it. "Where *were* you last night?"

He stood back up & crossed to the balcony. Behind the curtain, the sky was a pale heat-haze. A geometry of rooftops. Across the courtyard, a man & a woman were eating at a table, framed by pink & white *laurier rose*.

"I needed to think," Luce replied, barely above a whisper.

Hess's gaze followed the motion of a seagull as it arced across the sky. He listened to the sound of footsteps down below & recognised Ada coming across the street. She was carrying a basket. He toyed with the idea of relaying what she'd told him at breakfast, but thought better of it. He'd wait for the appropriate time, when the occasion presented itself. Unless Ada found the courage to tell Luce herself. But why not just leave it alone? And all that *demanding* crap. He was about to make a remark when Luce spoke.

"A Palestinian poet said, to kill a man in order to defend an idea isn't defending an idea, it's killing a man. Wolf's like that. If there was a revolution tomorrow, you'd be at the top of his list. He'd probably want to pull the trigger himself."

One more reason to be glad, he thought, wondering what he himself would do if he ever had an idea worth defending. But his thought was interrupted. There were voices coming from downstairs. It was Ada speaking with the woman at reception. The seagull he'd been watching swerved back up on a current of air & disappeared above the doorframe. He nodded to himself.

"You'll come down later, then?" he said.

Luce didn't answer. Instead she placed her hands flat on the bedspread.

13
dolce vita

First memory: the sun & light glinting on water. Naked. An eye wrenched into awareness. Sun, water. Everything else is vagueness without form. Things that have to be learned in order to be seen. In my memory I don't know how old I am. I'm simply an eye, hovering, disembodied. The world circulates above, without contours, in some remote, outer space. I imagine searching for something. What? Only by looking will I know. Fastforward: light flickering on a screen. A luminous halo separates the point of perception from the thing perceived, mobile & constantly shifting within its frame. The frame itself. The absolute.

Scene: A film being projected. Black-&-white. It begins with a close-up on a surface of water. The sun reflected, hovering, undulating, breaking apart & reforming again. Then pan back: in the foreground, the wheels & axles of an overturned car, visible above the waterline. To the left, children play on a stretch of beach. I'm vaguely reminded of the end of *La Dolce Vita*, when Marcello Mastroianni, in a white suit, kneels on the sand in a gesture of helplessness. In the background, a dozen drunk socialites ogle a sea monster hauled up onto the beach by fishermen.

But the two scenes have nothing to do with one another.

Except they're both in black-&-white. The sea evoking a shapeless melancholia. What's more, I can't tell if the first one's really a memory, or if I imagined it. How does it continue? Perhaps the camera closes in on the children. Three boys. One of them's holding an object in his hands. It could be a ball. A broken kite. The other two start chasing him. As they run across the sand, a flock of wading gulls takes to the air & settles again on the water further out. A detailed close up on the boys' feet sending up a fine spray of sand. Then the face of the boy running, mouth wide in laughter. Now we see all three, veering back towards the grassy dunes.

Throughout this scene the camera remains completely mobile & at the same time fixed. Everything appears to oscillate around it, cutting & zooming in & out. A series of broken perspectives miraculously assembled into a single, coherent impression. The sun on the water. The upturned car. The children playing on the beach. Time articulating itself without revealing its total form. Each movement supposes an object, but either we don't know what the object is or we can't guess what it signifies. Perhaps it doesn't matter. Perhaps that's the point.

Sun. Water. Car wreck. The game the children are playing.

This first scene would be followed by another. In sequence but not necessarily in succession. A man in a white suit leans against a railing with his back to the camera. He's gazing across the dunes onto the beach where the children are playing. The railing frames a café terrace on the marina. All of this is given immediately in a single establishing shot. The man watches the children running about. We can tell this because the camera gives us a view of the man's face, then a close-up of his eyes squinting into the sun, followed by a medium shot of the three boys chasing one another along the waterline. They veer back, disappearing behind the dunes, & we're left with the man.

The man turns his face in half-profile & we're immediately

able to recognise the missing connection to *La Dolce Vita*. But unlike Marcello Mastroianni, the man in the white suit is balding & wears a pair of square-rimmed glasses. His forehead's perspiring. He takes his glasses off & wipes them with a handkerchief he keeps in his right trouser pocket... *To hope for any kind of relief's pointless.* He directs these words at himself rather than at the camera, as if playing the role of a spectator who's both inside the frame & outside it. A dreamer & the observer inside the dream.

The camera cuts to a shot of the empty beach, the wreck, the sun low in the sky. Then the man in the white suit, shading his eyes from the sun with his hand. A moment later he turns. The camera follows him as he crosses the terrace to the café. A pair of glass doors swing open. We find ourselves looking as if into a cave at the interior of a typical 1980s seaside establishment. Padded stools. A zinc-topped bar. Display counters cluttered with junk. Moulded plastic chairs & tables. A row of coin-operated candy & bubblegum dispensers. Pinball machine in one corner.

The camera anticipates the man's movements. Suddenly we're inside the café, perspectives reversed, watching his silhouetted in the doorway. His face comes gradually into focus. Eyes. They move as if looking for something. We hear a shot. A car backfiring. The man turns & rushes down a stairway onto the pavement outside. A white convertible speeds away from the marina, past an open allotment. We see a woman behind the steering wheel. Black sunglasses, hair fanning behind her in the wind. Her shoulders are bare but we can't identify anything else about her. The man comes to a stop by the edge of the road, staring after the car. We suppose, knowing no more than this, that we've participated in some kind of drama whose details are familiar from many other films.

This more or less conventional scene then dissolves into

other, equally conventional scenes. A different man & woman at a restaurant table, conversing intimately, framed by a large window onto a busy street. Behind them a white convertible pulls up beside a kiosk. The woman looks at the man expectantly as the man turns to watch the driver rush from the convertible across the street into a hotel. The sound of car horns. We read in the man's gaze intimations of a cheap hotel room with a couple fucking. The woman seated opposite him, or the woman he's just seen running across the street? Both at once?

Cut to a scene on a beach: grey-&-white striped umbrellas. A close-up of a beachball rolling across the sand towards the water. A third woman, sitting on a deckchair, is squinting through the viewfinder of a camera at something far-off, undefined. The drama has enlarged, the number of observers multiplies. The camera, the intimate rendezvous of the couple in the restaurant, the woman in the car, the man in the white suit. Their order of appearance seems to dramatise an unstated idea. The question's how to proceed?

I amuse myself by sketching possible scenarios. Am I supposed to be the man in the suit? But the film's entirely capable of proceeding without me. In any case, I've always lacked the revenge-artist's passion for plot. Artifice rapidly loses its hold of actions & no longer constrains them. They find a life of their own. They impose their own rhythms, their own urgency & necessity. Things it'd take years to isolate & understand.

❁

Waiting's something I was never good at. It's after six. I can't remember what time Wolf's flight was supposed to get in. The itinerary's written down somewhere, but if I begin looking now I won't get it out of my head. And then what if the plane's late, if he missed his connection, or there's traffic out of Kiel? My anxiety's entirely pointless, but all anxiety is, unless you believe it's the only emotion that counts. I should go out, but I'm paralysed by the idea of running into someone I'll recognise. It's an absurd idea. On a drizzling October morning, when I haven't set foot in the place for fifteen years.

What comes next? You spend the night pacing a room. Sitting. Lying on a bed in which you can't sleep. Looking out the window. Staring at a mirror. A fleeting glimpse of someone, over your shoulder, naked on the carpet, on all fours. Marita's face. Offering herself with a sad hungry look in her eye. A ghost. Thinking of Ascher's bare feet. Hands, paint crusted round the fingernails. I pull the chair over to the desk & pick up the photographs. There have to be better ways of dealing with this. I look at the two pictures. The first in colour, the second in black-&-white. Is death easier to imagine with or without colour?

I have to keep reminding myself Ascher's really dead. That it isn't just the idea of him that's dead. That this's the reason I'm here, not for any other reason. That right at this moment bits of him are lying in the bag at the foot of the bed. That my being in this room has nothing to do with me. And yet it has everything to do with me.

When I first explained to Luce about Ascher, she didn't seem to understand. No, that's not it. I never attempted to explain anything. I was raving. Drunk. Putting the moment off for as long as possible. Or it was afterwards & I was hungover, then drunk again. And it suddenly hit me: *I can't feel anything.* Was it his death or my indifference that bothered me most? Then fast-forward: three days ago with Luce in Paris, facing one another across a table at the Rostand like that couple in the film inside my head. She'd held my hand. It was a curious gesture, because I could see it meant she felt sorry for me. How some people want you to believe you're judged in proportion to your insistence on being at the centre of every trial. It's the same now. I try to

98

imagine what Ascher would've done in my shoes, but it's a ridiculous idea. He'd never've been in my shoes.

Cut to: a dirty little room, heavy brown curtains, patterned wallpaper. Brown carpet with patches worn in a dozen places. A narrow steel-frame bed. Horsehair mattress stinking of sweat, piss. A grimy sink in the corner with a cracked mirror screwed to the wall above it. There're tiles & a dark mildewed patch beneath, where the pipes have leaked. A naked light-bulb dangles from a wire in the middle of the room which succeeds in exaggerating the gloom.

But why not have him standing at an open window, sunlight filling up the frame? September. The clamour of the wharfs. Lorries in endless succession up the ramps to the container yards. Stink of diesel, effluent, sea brine. It's an ordinary morning, life's going on. Ascher, with his mask-like face, turns from the window & sits on the exposed mattress. Patiently & with obvious intent, he takes a four litre can of petrol & pours it over himself. Without pausing, he strikes a match. Just the one, just once. A sudden rush of flame jets up around him. The open window acts as a flue, fuelling the fire as it spreads up the wallpaper, licking at the already fume-blackened ceiling. There's a crash. The exploding air in the petrol tin propels it off the bed & into the mirror above the washbasin. Shattering it.

14
Totem

Hess lay on his back in the water in a bodily cruciform. Arms outstretched, feet pointing horizon-wards. With eyes closed he lay there under the late morning sun, lulled by the echo of stones inched back & forth on the harbour floor. The sound of a continuous struggle, that'd gone on for as long as the tides. In his mind he was alone in some far off place. The eye's membrane like an embryonic sack. Something about to give birth. The swimmer in his womb-eye. Afloat in his Christ-body.

A pair of seagulls circled overhead. He heard their cries. Place & time: *Le Faubourg de Collioure*, 1905. Consider: being dead a hundred years, then made to come back, Lazarus-like. To see again through unchanged eyes the changed scene. Ghost-shapes hovering over everything like bits of overlapping celluloid.

I was dead & then I woke?

Head back-tilted, Hess opened his eyes. The sun, a vortex of light. Dazzling. Salt water stung his eyes. He blinked. By increments, an upside-down world, hazily. Of striped beach umbrellas, suspended in air. Bodies in motionless flight, hovering above. A host of reddened, half-naked seraphim. One hundred years ago, fishermen hauling in their catch. The ubiquitous stench of fish-gut. All of a sudden a cry went up at the water's edge. The shouts of children:

"Méduse! Méduse!"

Something washed-up. Formless. Decaying. Dead.

Hess rolled over in the water & shaded his eyes. A hundred years compressed into a hovering uncertainty. A flash of sunlight on the sea. & there, at precisely the spot above the beach where the pastry chef's son had painted it, the scene from which Hess now peered, propped beside an empty picture frame raised on a viewing stand for tourists to glop at. To see what Derain saw. He sketched a mental portrait: *Time reversed. See through dead men's eyes an unborn image of the living present!* And could the pastry chef's son have imagined a hundred years on, standing again in that place like an ogling idiot, perceiving the scene anew?

Hess cast his eyes along the beach taking it in by facets. Gulls streaked across the sky. *The most seductive thing about art,* Luce had written to him in one of her long incomprehensible emails, *is the personality of the artist himself. The fascination of genius.* Why people gave themselves up to a Creator, their personal God... *And if the pastry chef's son couldn't've envisaged us,* Hess thought, *could he nevertheless have invented us?* Like dough balls. If you put it that way, weren't they all just a consequence of some experiment to break apart the atom? Form & content? The good & the beautiful? Gestalt und Wirklichkeit? In a chain reaction from the first alchemy down to the imperceptible present? The lost tribe to the proverbial baker's dozen? Another shout went up.

"Méduse!"

Fugue-like voices pursued one another along the beach, till taken up by the wind & dispersed. Now echoed. Returning. Now re-divided. Scattered. Pursuing.

"Méduse! Méduse!"

Subject & counter-subject. Theme & variation.

At the tide mark, a throng of children had gathered around an older boy who held aloft the decomposed, translucent blubber of a large jellyfish on the end of a stick. *Tiens, Donatello au milieu des fauves...* They shouted. Jumped excitedly up & down. Rushed in circles. Darted. Arms flapping, necks craning.

"Méduse! Méduse!"

Blond Perseus exhibited his prize. Triumphant. Indulging the eager hoard. They pushed each other aside. They peered. Poking with curious or timid fingers. *Méduse!* they howled. And shimmied about. Hess waded through the shallow water. Eyed the blue-green shapelessness. Its tentacles like a decomposed ganglion. Jellied brain. Half-dissected genitalia. *Writhing serpents of green hair...* And those weird children dancing around it. Hollering before the totem of their savage god.

As he came out of the water, the crowd on the shore turned to stare at him. An interloper to their tribal mystery. The boy Perseus, too, holding the jellyfish on the end of his stick, gazed at him with puzzled expression. He reminded Hess vaguely of himself. Teleported to some mythological dimension of his own past. A boy with a stick, standing by the sea. Unaware that all around him the black waters enclosed mysteries he'd never want to learn the secret of. *The dark illimitable ocean...*

The boy with the stick raised his left hand & appeared to beckon. But he was merely shading his eyes, so as to read the belfry clock. Hess stood directly in line with it. And yet he was convinced some part of himself... Looking back through the boy's eyes... Like something nominally alive, turned to stone. An object sinking through time. Then everything slowed, began to move backwards. The arc of the boy's hand. The waves on the stones. The totem dance. *Snakehaired head...*

The boy with the stick turned away & walked up the beach, parting the throng of children. With the air of a Greek hero, he thrust the Gorgon's head in a rubbish bin. The children, curiosity sated, each went their own way among the pebbles & broken shells. From time to time they called to the mythical beast, as if to summon it back again. One would point at some undefined patch of water, another would cry speculatively:

"C'est une méduse?"

❁

Conscious of a scrutiny that wasn't directed at him, Hess stumbled up the beach, stones digging into his feet. Beneath a blue-&-white umbrella, a woman in green swimsuit, a shawl covering her shoulders, lay sideways on a towel. Luce had propped herself up on one elbow & was holding a sheaf of manuscript pages in her right hand. A wry expression hovering across her face as she flipped the pages. In the shade she could've been mistaken for a brunette. A trick of light.

He lay down heavily on the beach towel beside her & immediately closed his eyes, head resting on folded arms. Some moments later he heard Luce say something, too indistinct to tell what it was. Perhaps it was simply in his head. In a short while he drifted into a complicated sleep: he found himself alone on a railway siding at the end of dyke that ran between the sea & a shallow lagoon.

The scene was part of a recurring dream. He'd had the same dream just the night before. It continued now more or less from where it'd broken off. He'd left the railway platform & was walking along the tracks, the dry air hot in his throat. There were traces of a scrub fire ahead. Smoke still hung over the horizon. Each element stood out in uncanny detail. Their veracity startled him. Along the dyke, clumps of long yellow grass were bent over, as if by the wind, but in fact under their own weight. A ridge of scarred & deeply cracked clay ran the length of the earthworks, evidence of the outgoing tide. Rusted machine parts stood out of the lagoon. Concrete tank-traps. Sacks of rubbish embedded in the mud.

He was naked. The heat from the sun had blistered his flesh. He searched frantically for somewhere to shelter. In the middle of the lagoon was a set of white moulded plastic furniture. A table & two chairs, shaded beneath a blue-&-white striped umbrella. He ran towards it, stumbling down the embankment. No sooner had he begun wading into the lagoon bed than his legs sank deep into mud, stuck fast. On all sides, the muddy water churned with the thrashing of dying fish.

With a start, Hess woke. He felt something wet flutter across his face. When he opened his eyes he saw a girl was lying on a towel barely a metre from him. She'd just come out of the water & was still wet. It was the water dripping from her bikini as she arranged her towel that'd fallen on his face. His gaze moved along the length of her body to the tanned, boyish curves of her buttocks. Her lean thighs beaded with sea water. The image of the girl hovered behind the red of his eyelids as he drifted back into sleep. It kept coming apart, swelling, forming hollows & falling back in place again. In the interval of a few seconds he imagined kneeling beside the girl in the red bikini. Bending over her. Grazing his lips along her neck. Her breasts. The inside of her brown thighs. Then he jolted awake again. Rearranged himself, arms folded behind his head. Squinted. The clock-face in the tower of Our Lady of the Angels read just before noon.

Luce was speaking to him. He could see her mouth moving. She reminded him of the way his auntie looked when he'd had a fever once. Instead of a voice, there was a strange paradoxical music. Tranquilising, monotonous & vaguely dissonant. Which he could only just make out above the ringing in his ears. Reminding him, too, of the way, as a child, he'd tempt himself to defile his auntie's stockings & underwear. Then in a fit of guilt sought to undo what he'd done. He raised himself up on one elbow. Luce had stopped speaking & was now looking at him expectantly.

"I'm sorry..." he heard himself say.

Though he didn't know what it was he was sorry for. For not being able to understand her?

15
cardiogram

As ever the echo, the unexpected junction, is found only at polar extremes.

– Sergei Eisenstein

It happens like this: I see myself, lying on my back in the water, looking up at the sky. A hawk's circling high up. Two smaller birds are trying to chase it off, darting & diving. The hawk continues to circle, weathering the attack, drawing out the pursuit. Eventually the two smaller birds will exhaust themselves. The hawk will swoop down onto their undefended nest as the pair look on helplessly. I follow its descent. There's a commotion in one of the pines at the north end of the beach. Something tumbles to the ground. A fluttering of unformed wings, some limp & barely existing thing, as the guilty party steals away.

It's a real memory. But it comes to me like a dream. Something observable, detached, in which I'm nonetheless implicated. The anxiety symbolised in the hawk conceals a deeper sense of guilt. Guilt at the knowledge of what's about to happen. Being aroused by it. The helplessness of the two birds, the casual slaughter. In reality, I know my anxiety stems from a desire to see the two birds suffer. Because instead of defending the nest, they were defending an idea they themselves were at the centre of. But in the dream I'm punishing myself. I feel the weightless plunge of the chick falling to the ground. Punishing myself while providing an alibi. Because in reality, I'm the one who's survived.

✪

One day towards the end of August, during the *dies caniculares*, when the thermometers were fit to burst, a fleet of fire engines appeared outside Wolf's house. Smoke was billowing from the windows. Wolf's mother had fallen asleep in front of the TV, cigarette in hand. At the hospital, they kept her under a white oxygen tent. We envisioned the sort of cheap effects in Cinecittà B-films. Half-dissolved face & tortured limbs. Wolf wasn't allowed to see her, only a window to the room her shrouded silhouette lay in. The cardiogram, he said, sounded like a U-boat spiralling into the abyss. She lingered for several days without ever regaining consciousness. It was the smoke that killed her.

Wolf never believed his mother was really there inside that room with the cardiogram, the respirator, the oxygen tank. Just an echo chamber with shadows. Later he said it made him think of vapour trails left in the sky by jet planes, though he didn't know why. The smoke still coming off the charred window-frames, when we went back. The silence. The smell of wet ashes. It was like she'd been punished for the rat poison. Not because of Wolf, but because she'd tried to cheat the world by taking an easier way out.

After the funeral, I dreamt of Wolf's mother lying extended in her coffin. In my dream, the coffin was open & she was wearing an orange bikini with dark sunglasses & red lipstick. The fire hadn't disfigured but rather purified her. She was pristine, like a painted statue of the Blessed Virgin or a Warhol silk screen & not some shoddy corpse in a mortuary photograph. Pure celluloid embalmed in the flesh. *Virgo intacta.*

In my dream, the coffin was raised on trestles beneath the

open sky. In the background, black sand stretched away. The faint smell of ash mingled with perfume. A group of strangers stood around the coffin, faces perplexed, as if unable to make sense of something. The weather perhaps. Wolf stood at the foot of the coffin laughing silently to himself, as a pair of stiffs in labcoats lowered the lid. Soon it was going to be shut. A moment of solemnity came over everyone. A few hid their faces, the rest kept their eyes assiduously fixed on her body while avoiding her gaze. Wolf's mother knew nothing about all this, of course. In contrast to the undercurrent of hysteria running among the mourners, she remained calm to a fault. Her death was like a secret everyone was trying to keep from her.

In the foreground, a rectangular hole had been dug out of the sand. Obviously the coffin was supposed to be buried there. The tide was turning & water began pouring into the hole, cascading over the rim, without ever reaching the bottom. And all the while that melancholy tableau, hovering, like an image frozen on a TV screen. Beginning to dissolve in a haze of static. And gradually to disappear.

16
The Dead Woman

Because she couldn't bear the heat of the hotel room. And the narrow streets beneath the Miradou were cooler at that time of day, away from the crowds. Walls stuccoed indigo, sienna, Indian red. A stairway leading down. A fountain set at the foot of it, depicting a naked Venus surrounded by naiads. Window-boxes with hibiscus, gardenia, bougainvillea overflowing. Rooftops tilting across the alley, almost meeting. Adèle raised her camera & snapped the brightly mildewed Venus.

The place was unreal, allegorical almost. Balustrades patterned by volutes. A low barbican with crenellations. Terracotta. An embrasure blocked by dead leaves. The sea's cobalt through the balistrarias. Peering out from the darkness of the camera, it reminded her of someplace she might've dreamt once. Like a film you can't remember, only the fact of having seen it. Sometime. Somewhere.

Unaware that she was following, haphazardly, the exact path Luce had followed the night before, Adèle paused in a doorway framed with hanging plants, standing in the very spot. A cat mewed. Black & ginger. She took its photograph. Herself reflected in its eye. Conscious in her turn only of the light fixed within the lens, regulating the world into objects. And that this was how she saw things. The way the camera saw them.

Upon entering the Place 18 Juin, detachment became its inverse. Space crowded in, surrounded with a sudden onrush, turned inside-out, retreated again behind the viewfinder, shutter guillotine-like chopping the fleshy mass into pieces. Bodies in endless procession, avariciously stupid, made ever more nauseating by a raw seafood stench wafting from the vitrines along the strand, stuffed with perspiring lobster, octopus, fish pâté dressed with desiccated rind, parched fennel & fastidiously butchered dill.

❂

Clustered at the end of the strand, a retinue of buskers, hawkers, jugglers, tour agents & ice cream vendors. Pistachio, aniseed, rum raisin. A pair of human statues stood on makeshift pedestals, immobile, covered from head to toe in white paint, failing to attract an audience. The Statue of Liberty. Heliogabalus. Beneath an umbrella on a chair, a bored monkey in a red tuxedo chewed its tail searching for lice, a long chain from a collar around its neck. A midget wearing a sandwich-board leered insanely. *Promenade sur Mer*, the board said. Someone urged a brochure into her hand. She clutched her camera & pushed stoically on.

The end of the breakwater dropped off onto barnacle encrusted rock. Spiny black sea urchins. Broken wine bottles. Though deserted at that time of day. To her right, the Templar château jutting into the port. Left, Plage Boramar, every inch of it occupied. Framed by the medieval latrines in the high wall of Notre Dames des Anges, perched over the water. *Marinated in shit*, she thought. *How can they bear stewing in this heat? Just a few degrees more…*

The thought was enough to make her hyperventilate. But if she'd stayed inside at the hotel she'd only have ended up thinking of Louise. Recording her misery in the bathroom mirror. How many times had she photographed herself in the process of some kind of collapse, only to delete the evidence afterwards? Knowing if she stopped taking pictures the demons would just take another form. The choice between Hell &

Purgatory. *Which one are you in now?*

The camera's eye surveyed the scene. Thinking perhaps she'd recognised Louis in the crowd, a redhead in a green swimsuit, she glanced up from the viewfinder. But she was mistaken. Her eye returned the viewfinder. The woman's body now simply a body. It possessed no other individuality than that bestowed by the lens. Allowing the zoom to linger over the woman's body, her neck, breasts, thighs, almost as if she was caressing them. *As if* it was Louise. And if she closed her eyes, touching her, how would she know? She held her breath. The viewfinder went dark.

When she looked up, a man was standing directly in front of her, staring. Abruptly she turned, crossed back along the breakwater. She paused & glanced over her shoulder to see if the man was following her. But he was standing in the same place, eyes fixed on something in the distance. She followed his gaze. Across the bay, a unit of légionnaires from the garrison were lined up on a pontoon, in black scuba gear. Half-newts, half-men. An inflatable sped past. The air tasted of diesel & sea-salt.

She swallowed hard, letting the camera drift up to the tower at the crest of the hill, hypnotically immobile above the Moulin. Then out past the headland in a continuous arc. The shape of the Cadaqués ferry through the haze. In the foreground, a wooden barque was manoeuvring past the buoys & turning its prow towards the harbour mouth. Zooming in on the sail. All around it, the reflections of the yachts lying at anchor in the razzle of light on water.

She adjusted the aperture. Snapped. Then, an afterthought, remembered the brochure still clutched in her left hand. The front of it showed the same kind of barque, gaudily immaculate in blue, yellow, red. They were called llaguts, bouares, sardinales, it said. *These boats, made of holm oak for the hull & pine for the mast, have a triangular sail called a latine & have been used for anchovy & sardine fishing since the middle of the fourteenth century. From Collioure, large quantities of salted sardines were dispatched to other countries. In 1466, Louis XI exempted the inhabitants from paying salt tax, because they needed to salt fish...* How very benevolent, she thought, that Louis XI must've been.

✪

That morning, returning from the markets, Adèle had found Louise in her room. Embarrassed at first, surprised. She'd cried & began apologising, not knowing what it was she was apologising for. But the look on Louise's face silenced her. Standing in the middle of the room, a statue. Adèle went to her & for a long time they held each other wordlessly.

What disturbed their silence was the voice of a child from the doorway. A little blond-haired boy was standing there, staring up at them with eyes wide, pointing & saying *mamapapa*. Brow furrowed, head tilted quizzically, as if posing a question & making a statement at the same time. They'd both turned to look at him, astonished by the sudden apparition...

"Mamapapa," he repeated,

Laughing, Adèle stooped down to offer the boy a nectarine from her basket.

"Brugnon!" he exclaimed, holding the fruit aloft in triumph. Then smiled broadly at them & scampered back down the corridor. "Brugnon! Brugnon!"

"What a strange child!" Louise said.

"Aren't all children like that? It's us who seem strange to them. They can't figure us out! "

"Mamapapa?"

"Exactly."

But now Adèle could feel the sun reddening her skin. She'd forgotten to bring a hat. The heat was making her feel dizzy. Across the bay, the frogmen were plunging backwards into the

114

water, like a film reel running the wrong way. Watching them made her feel even hotter. The terrace overlooking Plage d'Avall hardy seemed crowded at all. She decided to try for it. There were palm trees with shade. And awnings. To get there she had to navigate the promenade under the château walls. She shielded herself behind her camera, photographing the rock pools. A child's shoe in the water.

Plage d'Avall was separated from the terrace by high wall. She climbed some steps. Paused to photograph the children's playground. An old customs tower & ancient carousel. Galloping unicorns undulated surreally on striped poles to the sound of cracked accordion music. The carrousel was like something out of Salvador Dalí. As she zoomed & tracked, the baroque scrollwork became dripping clocks, eggs, horses, genitalia, menacing beasts. She wondered how the children weren't terrified to ride it. But then, there weren't any children. The carrousel was empty. A music box playing to the sea.

She gazed back at where she'd been. A figure on the breakwater. Click. And what if, she thought, someone else right now was watching *her?* Taking *her* picture? Who'd been watching her all along? Compiling a dossier? The watcher watched? The ferry to Cadaqués, she could see, had docked & was already sounding its horn, due to depart again. She'd wanted to take it, but Louise kept promising they'd drive.

Louise, forever caught in her book, had wanted to see a particular view of the town, painted in 1910 by André Derain. In imitation of Braque imitating Cézanne. Adèle attempted a mental picture. Cap Creus. The Camel, the Eagle, the Anvil, the Dead Woman, the Monk, the Lion's Head. Dalí's museum with its flaming giraffes & Pirelli tyres. The paladin of kitsch. Now Dalí, too, stood for how dependent she'd become. *It's not healthy*, she told herself, fidgeting with her lens cap. She scanned back through that morning's photos. There was one of Louis leaning against a window, taken while she was looking away…

"Why not come to the beach?" Louise had asked.

But without giving her time to find the words, Louise had turned & come across to her, & kissed her on the lips. The way she did to evade contradiction. To be denied. And then she'd gone into the bathroom to get her swimsuit. And Adèle had taken her basket & slipped out, to avoid the recriminations. Was it really Hess that bothered her? And just now, had she really wanted to find Louise on the beach? Her right hand slid unconsciously across her abdomen. *Does she know?*

✪

A continuous stream of traffic made its way along rue de la Démocratie. Behind it, the Faubourg. Shuttered windows facing the sun. Finding a seat in the shade, Adèle took the morning's newspaper from her shoulder-bag & spread it on the table. There, again, on the front page, war was being declared. Israeli forces had penetrated in Southern Lebanon in an effort to recover two soldiers abducted by Hezbollah. A captioned photograph of an Israeli tank crew illustrated the story. *L'armée israélienne s'est positionée dans le Sud-Liban après la violente attaque du Hezbollah dans laquelle deux soldats israéliens ont été enlevés et sept autres tués.* Three subordinate headings continued the story without adding anything:

Le Hezbollah ouvre un deuxieme front contre Israël…

Un enlèvement condamné à Washington et à Moscou…

Israël intensifie les operations dans la Bande de Gaza...

A waiter, trussed in a burgundy waistcoat no doubt insufferable in the heat, came over & she ordered a glass of citron pressé. She watched him disappear inside the café & then continued reading. Halfway down the page was an unrelated article about one Captain Alfred Dreyfus, a Jew. It was the hundredth anniversary of his exoneration, wrongfully accused of treason. At a ceremony marking the occasion, President Chirac addressed an audience including several of Dreyfus's descendants. The President made a finely polished speech. *Like the proverbial turd*, she thought. *La réhabilitation de Dreyfus, c'est la victoire de la République. C'est la victoire de l'unité de la France...* Now they could all sleep at night with their clear consciences. *Quelle merde!*

She turned the page. Bomb blasts had rocked India's financial capital, blamed on Islamic extremists. Iran's nuclear dossier was doing the rounds of the UN Security Council. George W. Bush was in Berlin to discuss the "Iraq Problem." The world was a mess, no sign of a miracle on the horizon. How long could things could go on like that before the whole sham came apart, without ceremony? Thinking at that moment of Wolf, saying how the situation was untenable. And demonstrating the truth of his own words by getting up & leaving for Beirut.

It'd happened so quickly. She woken up one day & he was gone. As suddenly, she reminded herself, as he'd appeared. That was all. And then a letter (finally) from Louise. Half-accusation, half-begging her to come to France. Because she (Louise) was in the midst of some crisis, which she almost always was. And unlike the crisis of the world at large, maybe she could help. But she'd resisted. *Untenable*, she'd thought. *And isn't everything untenable?*

It was only because Louise had kept urging, insisting, that she'd agreed to come. But no sooner had she arrived than Louise no longer needed her. And that stupid book. And now Hess, putting in his obligatory appearance. And there was going to be a war in Lebanon. And of course Wolf was in Lebanon. And on top of it all she was certain she was pregnant.

She pushed the paper aside. *Things are bad enough, without letting your imagination make them any worse.* Afraid of all the many types of loneliness. But there was no need to discuss loneliness. It was a waste of time. What Wolf had said, almost exactly in those words. Perfunctory. Alienated from his own predicament. *Nobody ever really died of loneliness.* The way he'd said it made her feel like a stone, a lump of petrified wood. The type of thing children keep in jars of ethanol, so they'll stay pristine & glisten in the light.

The waiter at last brought the citron pressé & a tall jug of ice water. Adèle smiled wanly while he attempted small talk, waiting for him to go. As soon as he had, she poured water into her glass & tasted the result. Winced. Stirred in a sachet of cane sugar. Except for the tables facing the harbour, the café was empty. Sure nobody was looking, Adèle reached into her bag & withdrew a vial of white pills. Shook three onto the palm of her right hand & swallowed them with the diluted lemon. Even like that, they left a sour taste.

To her dismay she noticed the waiter was leaning back against the bar scrutinising her unabashedly. Taking medication in public always made her nervous, as if exposing herself to a general opprobrium. *He probably thinks he knows my weakness now. He'll come over & say something, try to hold it over me.* Like Wolf...

"You take too many of those," he'd said.

"I can't think otherwise, you know that."

118

She'd felt like an idiot justifying herself that way. Him telling her how she needed to take responsibility. For what? *What do you know about my sense of responsibility?* But she'd simply nodded, like an admonished child. It was all a conspiracy, to make people accept things the way they are. *Anaesthetised*, he'd meant to say. *Meaning stupid.* But of course she knew. And that was *precisely* the reason she couldn't do otherwise.

But it wasn't what she'd said. Instead she'd told him how much she admired his selflessness, always committed to helping the oppressed. While thinking: *I'm a victim too. Even you're a victim. You just can't see it because of your ridiculous saviour complex. That's your drug, your opium, social salvation. And you peddle it anywhere people will buy it.* Hardly better than a pusher, she'd decided afterwards. Feeding a sense of insufficiency, powerlessness, alienation, anger, exclusion. But when the drug wore off, when the revolution turned cold, he'd be just like every other pusher.

She stared at her hands to see if they were shaking. *What do I care about that?* she thought. Then: *He'll come back. You'll have the child. It's not his fault there's going to be a war.* And she imagined his voice telling her to wake up, that she'd been asleep. Dreaming. But she wasn't asleep. She was fully conscious. Only she didn't know *why*. Did she need a reason? And she imagined saying to him life wasn't about *why*, it was about whatever happened. *Two particles join. Become one. Divide again.*

Just as her own existence seemed fractured, barely held together, given proof by the ghost inside the camera. The still point inside the chaos. Which in the end appealed to her sense that even *her* existence was too deliberate, *too composed*, simply to've been a molecular accident. Could all the fluctuating currents of life & pre-life be reduced to this? The flow of blood reversing in the foetus' heart at birth? The *foramen ovale* & *ductus arteriosus*? Was everything really just incoherence put in a different light? As arbitrary & senseless as that?

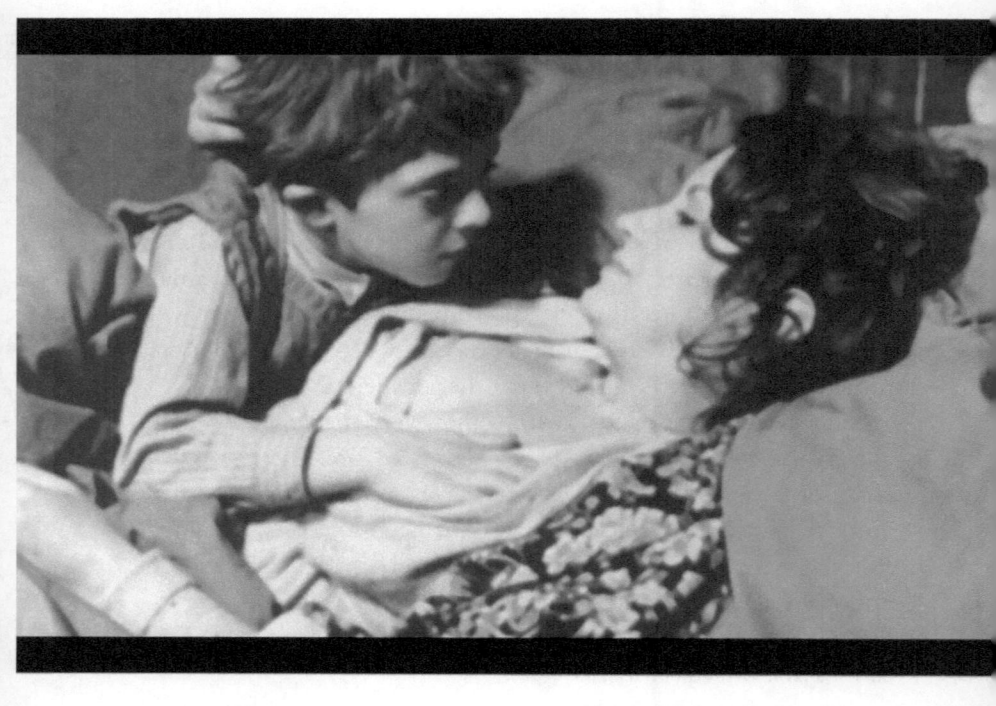

17
ramapithecus

Each human generation carries
within itself all the previous
generations, & appears like a
foreshortening of universal history.
– José Ortega y Gasset

Amber, emerald, sapphire, ruby. Auntie Freude, born in the East
& raised in refugee camps, hung coloured glass beads in the
kitchen window. They caught the sun, cast prismed light across
ceiling & walls. She's still there, how I remember her, watering
the rosemary in red ceramic Devo pots on the windowsill, flames
of light shimmering & darting. Every summer, how she'd sew
rosemary into the pillow cases, perfuming the linen. The same
perfume on beige stockings left to dry in the laundry. The scent
of rosemary has always aroused in me the imagined pleasures of
an older woman.

✿

My auntie's house was a narrow two-story affair, blue awnings
over windows & cluttered back garden. I lived there ever since I
can remember. There was a birdbath hidden among backyard
shrubbery, like a chamber pot on a wrought iron stand thick with
cobwebs. The water, algal-green. In the summer, mosquitoes,
frogs & dragonflies. A red tricycle with rusted wheels, upside
down, lay tangled into the undergrowth.

My auntie had a workroom behind the stairs, where she
tailored clothes for the women in the neighbourhood. A

cardboard dressmaker's dummy stood in the middle of the small room, surrounded by mirrors in which it multiplied in ways strange & sinister. Eye glued to the keyhole, I'd watch while she fitted the lady from next door. Frau Schöneborg. Who wore a girdle to keep her flesh in place. Or else the young store owner's wife from the bungalow at the end of our street. Unlike Frau Schöneborg, this one had long thin legs & didn't wear a girdle, but she had no breasts either.

Auntie Freude liked to tell stories about people I didn't know & who seemed invented just to entertain me. I found the stories hard to follow & preferred staying up to watch old films on the portable black-&-white that sat atop a locked cabinet in her bedroom. Only later I learned the cabinet held the bottles of gin which for years she drank in secret, hidden among the petticoats & underwear, perfume & talc.

We'd soak up UFA-era Ernst Lubitsch & Gerhard Lamprecht flicks, Pola Negri almost always in the lead. Or Hollywood standards like *Sunset Boulevard* & *The Maltese Falcon*. Falling asleep side-by-side long after midnight. I remember once, head against her arm, gazing at a swirling pattern on her negligee. Realising later it wasn't a pattern at all, but a ring of dark hairs snaking about her nipple, visible through the fabric.

Afterwards I dreamt recurrently of my auntie's breast. To smell the rosemary mingled with the salt of perspiration on her skin & taste it. I longed to be nearer to the feminine mystery. These dreams were complicated by images from stories she told about the Amazons. I wondered if it was true they cut off their right breast. My mother, I knew, had suffered from cancer. A double mastectomy. But the cancer had already spread. It made me ashamed of my arousal. I read somewhere once that a mother's the only woman who loves a man selflessly. But I knew that wasn't always true.

✻

The two sisters grew up in the shadow of one of those dreary, repressive Protestant religions, sleeping with a bible under their pillows. Chalk & cheese, she said. Auntie Freude, the elder of the two, had grown up at the end of the War, in the retreat from the Red Army. Her sister, a blonde, athletic, popular with the boys, came after. Their father was an engineer in the Statistical Office who disappeared in the chaos. A court in Munich finally declared him dead in 1956. All this I gleaned from slim albums, certificates, bundles of letters my auntie kept at the back of her dressing table.

How they'd survived after the War, I never knew. Auntie Freude always despised the nostalgic bric-a-brac people back then surrounded themselves by, to ease their War-guilt. The national preoccupation with kitsch & death. History belonged in the wastebasket. There were no porcelain geese over her mantelpiece in flightless formation. Only a framed reproduction of the Madonna Litta, with the face of that sinister man-child at the Virgin's breast.

✻

The actual world seems far off, remote from these terrains of memory. The everlasting calm before the storm. Back in the summer when Wolf's mother died. The three of us, straddling our bicycles on the street in front of the house, smoke gusting through windows shattered by the heat. The fire engines late to arrive from wherever. A smell of sodden ashes hanging in the air. People milling about. None of them seeming to notice us.

Wolf & Ascher stayed at my auntie's house that night. Listening to the frogs in the yard. We knew it was the end. A premonition of the obvious. The very next day, Wolf's relatives came & took him back to Aachen, as they'd done before when his mother attempted suicide. It was eleven years before I saw him again, though I never stopped thinking about him. Why'd she do it? I pictured him over & over, like Peter Fonda in *Easy Rider*. The graveyard scene. Where he climbs up into the arms of a statue of the Virgin Mary & cries: *You're such a fool mother, I hate you so much!*

Not long after, I was sitting in my auntie's kitchen watching the water boil on the stove. The window with the glass beads. The grey humid rain-swept sky. There was a bowl of sesame & caraway seeds on the kitchen table. For some reason this detail stands out. I was trying to separate the sesame seeds from the caraway seeds. It was a pointless, slightly idiotic task. And all the while, occupying my thoughts, was the sound of the water boiling in the saucepan my auntie had left on the stove.

❂

Sea, rain, humidity. The mystery of water being liquid then steam, with nothing between. Or ice. Liquid, solid, vapour. Like flicking a switch, & suddenly steam was water, was ice. Maybe it wasn't true. Or not always true. Maybe there were conditions under which the processes varied. Or only the values. The way our teacher tried to explain why ice forms on the surface of a lake, & not at the bottom. Because as it gets chilled by the wind, by the nuclear winter, water gets heavier, convecting downward. But at four degrees everything reverses, the cold water spirals to the top & keeps getting colder. Till it freezes.

The Ice Age was something I'd read about in the *World Atlas*. Auntie Freude said there was no mention of it in the Bible. Only the Great Flood. Noah's Ark. Keeping to the facts. According to the atlas, the Ice Age was when Neanderthals made tools, hunted & lived in caves near Düsseldorf. Ramapithecus begat

Australopithecus begat Homo Erectus begat Neanderthal. And Neanderthal begat Cro-Magnon, who begat us. Like steam turning to liquid turning to ice, & nothing between. Nothing that was Homo Erectus & Neanderthal. No Piltdown Man with his wrong jawbone to prove the missing link. Evolution being punctual, not gradual, darkly revolving in silent activity. The law of catastrophe, not transition.

Was that what old man Darwin meant by survival of the fittest? And had the fittest survived, in their Promised Land? Or were the survivors simply the ones who'd made it to the next stage by pure happenstance? By grace of no higher power? Was history nothing but a dark prologue to some final cataclysm? Night of the Long Knives? Kristallnacht? Night of the Counting of Years…? And what did it mean if evolution passed no judgement? Unpurposed, brought to pass by furious black winds of perturbation? Had humanity come about as just one obtained element of the eternal conflagration, & not for any other reason? Was that the truth? What stood, then, between the Bible's God of plague & pestilence, & Adolf Hitler, if not an arbitrary adjustment in the cosmic law?

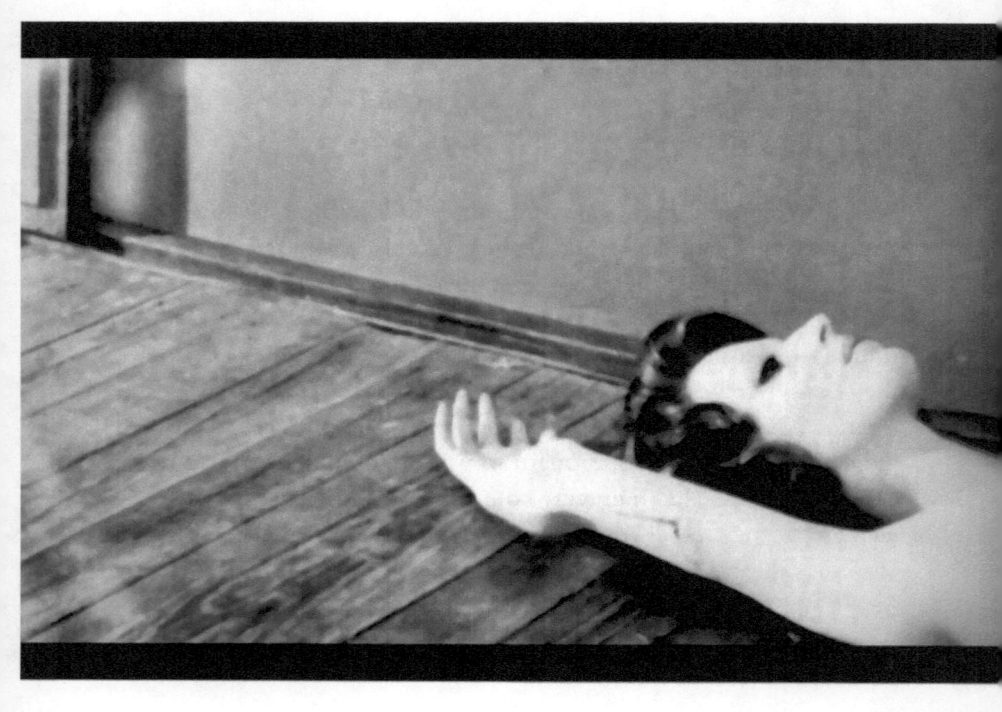

18
In the Direction of the Sea

Hess lay in a sweat listening to the voices circulate around him in the midday heat.

"It's as though you're describing something that isn't real."

A woman's voice. Hess zeroed in on it, to discover it belonged to a brunette, lying nearby on a canvas deckchair like a Modigliani nude, one arm bent above her head, a paperback dangling from her hand. Her interlocutor was a man in his early thirties. Balding. Tanned. Rectangular black-framed glasses. Who, as she spoke, began making the gestures of somebody preparing to stand up.

The place where they were sitting was shaded by a large blue-&-white umbrella, barely a metre from the water's edge. They were surrounded by similar umbrellas. Sunbathers. Someone reading a newspaper. A boy rubbing oil into a woman's back. An elderly man asleep on a fold-up wooden chair with transistor radio playing.

The woman on the deckchair was at that moment the spitting image of the actress in Passolini's *Teorema*. The scene, Hess thought, where she's lying at the top of the stairs. First in a bathing suit, then naked. Waiting for Terrance Stamp to come up & make love to her. Despite, or even because of her nudity, she was more like the effigy of a woman than an actual woman. Something about the arrangement of her body. Too mannered, overwrought. As if she'd given it a great deal of consideration & yet somehow failed to achieve the intended purpose. And was now attempting to compensate through a type of bodily overstatement.

Hess imagined the catalogue entry to accompany her image: *The modelling of the torso creates a tangible plasticity which stands out from the decorative surroundings...* He wondered what she'd been referring to. Something the man beside her had said? Something in the book she was reading? Herself? *It's as though you're describing something that isn't real.* The man had already stood up & was now walking away in the direction of the terrace. He wore a pair of crumpled white trousers & no shirt, a linen jacket slung over one shoulder. When he reached the terrace the man stood momentarily surveying the tables before moving off beneath the shade of the awnings & out of sight.

Hess tried to make out what she was reading. He strained to decipher what was written on the cover of the book the Modigliani woman was reading. Balkans? No. Bulgakov. *The Master & Margarita.* He wondered if there'd ever been a film with a woman reading a Russian novel on a beach. Probably. His eyes traced the dark contours of her breasts, shoulders, face. Something oddly dislocated about her figure. As if her arms, legs, head, torso had all been arranged in receding perspective, yet at the same time suspended in depthless immediacy. A figure composed entirely of surface effects. Planes. Geometries in collision. Something, he thought, that isn't real.

Hess pushed himself up onto his elbows, squinting across the bay at the rocky outcrop on the opposite shore. Luce had left her manuscript lying on her towel, a large pink & grey stone serving as a paperweight, though there wasn't even the hint of a breeze. She must've gone up to the terrace, he thought, for a drink. He glanced back in the direction the man had gone just a moment ago, then down at the manuscript. It suddenly occurred to him he didn't know his wife at all. She was just as unknown to him, in a way, as that woman lying there reading Bulgakov.

And what, he thought, spurred by a momentary inspiration, *if they really were the same woman? The same person existing at different times but in the same place?* The idea vaguely astonished him. Of course, yesterday someone entirely different would've been sitting here, exactly where I am, & perhaps it'll be the same tomorrow. But what if we were all in the *same* time, an eternal *singular* time, like images in multiple exposure? Different frames overlapping, inhabiting the same space, only invisible to one another?

He began in his head to sketch a scenario for a film, in which the lives of two strangers, living a century apart, somehow converged, became one. A mysterious synchronicity, determining that everything they'd ever done was identical in all fundamental respects. So that between them, between those two repetitions, time would contract, fold, join, becoming facets of a single instant *across* time. Like montage. The awareness of the one interceding in the other. Till the two actually *were* identical. Existing in both times simultaneously.

Hess dragged upright, took a few painful steps across the hot pebbles to the water's edge where he crouched down to splash cold water on his face & neck, before letting himself down into the shallows. The sun was approaching its zenith, the shadows their antipodes. Hess's legs stuck out in the water, reddened & vaguely shapeless. From the distance, the drone of an aircraft engine. Hess blinked up at the sky. A white single-prop Cessna was flying low around the headland, heading up the coast. Then it banked, flying directly towards the beach, before banking again. Behind it a long yellow banner trailed, advertising lemon soda. GIN & *KES* FOREVER.

He swam out a short distance, floating on his back, the sun burning his face, & closed his eyes. The water was cool, almost cold, despite it being the hottest July on record. It vied with the war for headline space on the newsstand.

Trente-Trois Departements en Alerte
contre la Canicule

Six hundred sick & elderly dead in the suburbs of Paris alone. Slaughtered by the heat. *Blame it on Sirius. Too close to the sun.* Perhaps the world was approaching the end sooner than expected. Apocalypse. The epoch of Hell. Better to make it six thousand. Or sixty thousand. Or six hundred thousand. Or six million. Everything adjusted upwards. How great would be the final reckoning? Hess had no answer. Did he care? Probably he didn't. He lay on his back & felt his emptiness buoy him. The world could burn, but he couldn't picture himself in it. He had no use for such a world. The world was just an idea, an image, that passed through him like the motion of the water.

Your a stone. Feel yourself sinking. Deeper. Now count. One. You're sinking into a deep sleep. Two. A pleasant warmth is flowing over you...

The sea practiced its hypnosis on him. Light glinting all around. He could dissolve at any moment, rising & gently falling on waves of celluloid. And he thought: *What if none of this's real?* Then, from nowhere, Wolf's voice. As if responding to a summons. A lost spirit walking the earth at midday. *The disappearance of reality,* the voice said, *is more real than reality itself.* Were those really his words? *The disappearance of reality...* But the truly revolutionary idea, he thought all of a sudden, wasn't that the world was submerged in illusion. That was obvious. But that without illusion, *without* the disappearance of reality, *nothing was real.*

Man with his profound sense of destiny, written in the twinkly stars. Zodiacs that existed only from where he could see them. *The Earth turns & our constellations spell out the old suffocating forms against the older formlessness.* Man & his deep cosmic intuition. The one idea. The collective delusion. The necessary order.

Truth by sidereal motion. And all Wolf's talk of revolution, just another way of spinning out the reel, keeping the dream from flickering out. The returning childhood ghost. The dead voice that sucked the life out of everything. Ingesting it the way the sea ingests the swimmer...

Hess rolled over, face-down in the water. He let his body go limp, arms down-hanging, sunlight refracted across the rocks below. *And what if I really were to drown, right now? For whom would that be real?* He closed his eyes. Drifted. He counted to a hundred before coming up for air. Gasped. And found a weirdly distorted face looking down at him. A hand reaching. It was a dwarf with goggles holding a piece of bread, shoulders barely above the water. The tied had carried Hess into the midst of a school of fish. He could feel their slick bodies stirring the water, butting his legs. And when he looked around him, the surface was alive with the silver glinting of their scales. Fish beaks snapped at the dwarf's bread. And close by, a piece of clear plastic in the water, wrapping & unwrapping itself.

The woman who a moment ago had been reading Bulgakov arched both arms over her head before plunging into the water. She passed him, executing the obscure, tortured rite of the butterfly stroke. A surreal contortion of the body as it heaved in & out, arms outstretched, torso suspended, like the hallucinated piscine body of something demi-human, half-myth. Redolent of those bare-breasted figures crucified on galleons' prows, vaulting the waves. Wide-eyed. Mane flung back. Water fanning from arms like the wings of a carrion bird.

His eyes followed the apparition out to the line of yellow buoys where the swell of the open sea rose in the harbour's mouth & obscured her from view. He lay back down in the water, thinking about the story in Bulgakov's novel. The midnight bride. He tried to picture the woman's eyes. Modigliani eyes. Dark. Epicanthine. & the man in the glasses, reaching across & grasping one of her exposed breasts in his hand. Then, like someone in an allegory, pointing with his other hand in the direction of the sea. Saying: *The reasons don't matter. It's what can't be turned into reasons that decides our actions. Everything else is just an alibi...*

He closed his eyes. Drifted. And almost immediately began to dream the same scene on the beach. But instead of the man & the Modigliani woman, it was Luce with her right hand pointing, & him sitting beside her. And instead of pointing at the sea, she was pointing at a girl in a red bikini, lying on the rocks with a primitive shrine built around her. A solemn procession of children down the beach, led by the boy with the jellyfish crucified on a stick. The girl lay there mannequin-like, one arm rigidly outstretched above her head. Eyes blank. Lips parted. Legs spread in a type of inertia of availability. Hess's gaze caressed her body then guiltily returned to her face. Only it wasn't the girl's face now, but Ada's, set as though moulded from plastic in a look of nauseated contempt. He wanted to spit at her. But something caused him to jerk around, in time to see the Modigliani woman soaring from the water, an angry Sphinx, as the tide surged, about to swallow him.

Hess blinked in panic. The hot sun burned his upturned face. Gulping salt water, he struggling to keep his head above water. The Modigliani woman was nowhere in sight. Beneath her umbrella, Luce was watching him. Feebly he raised a hand as if to wave.

19
endlösung

We unconsciously seek for the
principles & dogmas appropriate to
our temperament, so that in the end
it appears as though these principles
& dogmas had created our character
& given it firmness & assurance:
whereas what has happened is
precisely the reverse.
– Friedrich Nietzche

Nothing matters & then, when it's too late, everything matters. Not satisfied with being cynical, our bad faith seduces us to greater acts of credulity towards our own disavowals. History, unable to be that fabric of truths we were once constrained to believe in, becomes an alibi. For the present, everything depends on focusing uniquely on the task at hand. Work & thereafter, redemption. You could say it's a national characteristic. When we're not examining our puny souls. In any case, it won't be long now. The sky outside's almost white. It's time I put a few things in order. Made preparations. But there's really nothing to prepare, is there? Wolf'll arrive, we'll do what we came here to do, & that'll be that. And afterwards? Truth is, I'd prefer to've washed my hands of the entire business at the start. Delaying as long as possible. Three months. After fifteen years, what's three more months?

In the first place, I never wanted to come back. I've got my reasons. And now this. Wolf insisted I call Marita, speak to her. She called me. We spoke. What was there to say? I knew what she was thinking, behind the words. But she kept it to herself.

Wolf had got her to sign for what was left of Ascher after the crematorium. She rented a locker at the Altona Bahnhof. She'd been en route to Copenhagen anyway, living with her mother again. She mailed the locker key to me in Prague. That was Wolf's idea, too. It meant I couldn't back out. Ascher's remains now rest in a carry-bag, at the foot of the bed. His ghost hasn't stirred the whole time. His presence here doesn't disturb me. It's my own presence that disturbs me.

Only children believe in a world where everything nasty & disagreeable can simply be made to disappear. Die Endlösung. The final solution in reverse. Wolf used to berate me for lacking a political conscience. Did it mean I believed in nothing? When it comes down to it, it's as simple as this: politics for Wolf was & always has been a sadistic little boy's adventure. An endless erotic struggle to the death. A cruel naked desire that could never be satisfied, never be resolved one way or the other. Because death itself was the final victory. Humanity's existence, appalling as it is, as uncorrectable & brutal & stupid & beautiful, had nothing to do with it. Politics is a cold, deadly, seductive narcissism. The coldest, deadliest, most seductive of all.

Do I believe what I'm saying? I don't know. I neither believe nor disbelieve. I can only commit to learn by my mistakes & make adjustments. But who ever really does? And what's a political conscience anyway? Words like that have a habit of sounding self-righteousness. Semantics. You call something politics which's really just an opportunity to elevate an inner dispute into a paradigm for the species. A perfectly centred, childlike ego filling the universe. The agenda's always about seizing power however you dress it up. Why Marx theorised while Lenin went & got his laundry done.

Of course, when we were young & stupid, it all looked different. Our whole world view came second-hand from films. School was just about was getting your name spelt right. As I got older, more & more of the films on offer were American. It was a long time before I ever saw anything by Syberberg or Ottinger, whose politics was incomprehensible to a generation weaned on Spielberg. The directors I came to admire were completely marginalised back then. I had no idea how deep the margin went.

❂

Like a film with all the low points edited out, the summer days strung together into one long continuous vacation of the soul. The Cold War was ending & we were supposed to be smack-bang in the middle of it. But it happened without us. Somewhere, not so far away, the world had changed & our long summer was history already. Everything up to that point was drawn into a different focus. What we'd been, what we'd become. In fact, the messages were empty, *nothing* had happened. But from the dark age after Hiroshima (mon amour), how were we to see it?

Rewind: Ascher, squatting with his back against a rock, drawing his thoughts in the sand with a short stick. He'd always been an artist. His sketchbook full of menacing caricatures. Everything he drew was dark & neurotic, but no more dark & neurotic than the world was. He had this ability to model tiny figures from bird shit while we sunbathed at the foot of the caves, listening to old cassettes on a portable tape deck. *Go Rimbaud, do the Watusi…*

We smoked Luckies & generally bummed around, but it wasn't so interesting without Wolf. If he'd been there, we might've started something with the kids from the houseboats. Or cooked up some sort of scheme. Or blagued sodas from Frau

Wenzel. As the months passed I saw how Ascher's chest was gradually being covered in scars. There were just these thin, spidery pink lines flawing his tan. If I asked, he'd just shrug. I figured later he cut himself with a razor blade. Cigarette burns on the inside of his arms, too. He started wearing shirts. It was almost September, anyway. The Indian summer still lay ahead, but the days had grown shorter & evenings cooler, & things weren't quite the same anymore.

❁

About that time a dark-haired girl called Marita started hanging around the beach. Older than we were, she was the twin of Eva Mattes & didn't seem bothered by anything we did. Ascher turned her into a surrogate for Wolf, shadowing her around. Maybe that's when I figured something was up. Over a period of weeks his obsession grew. It brought out the evil in me. Whenever Ascher wasn't looking, I upset his arrangements.

Marita still looked like a kid, but on the inside it was different. We made-out at every opportunity. But when we started doing it for real she let me think it was my big idea. She knew all the tricks & had this inhuman capacity to never be bored. First we just frigged each other, like the musclemen on the rocks. As things progressed we'd slip down into the caves & suck each other & eventually fucked. She instructed me how to do it the way men did with each other. So she wouldn't get pregnant.

Maybe she just preferred being fucked that way. Maybe she'd been taught to prefer it. After, we'd run out to the channel & swim or just lie in the sand, letting it stick to us. Sometimes we did it while Ascher was drawing only a couple of metres away. Marita seemed to think that was funny as hell. She liked to be watched. I can imagine how it would've tortured Ascher if he'd known. But he had, hadn't he? Marita told us how she spied on her old lady doing it with the Dane. Maybe that was only half the story. The Dane was a day-labourer who lodged on their houseboat. Ascher had a quiet hatred of him. He was a huge man, the size of a door, with a shaved head. An Aztec sun symbol was tattooed on the back of his skull. The Eye of God. He must've had an enormous prick from the stories I heard.

Years later, in Berlin, I happened across a film about a Bulgarian immigrant in Hamburg. It reminded me of Marita & the Dane. As the story went, the Bulgarian married this girl who only let him have anal intercourse with her. Accompanied, it was duly noted, by savage neck-biting. Finally the Bulgarian was driven to shoot her with a rusty WWI pistol. When the cops arrested him, he tried to tear his wrists open with his teeth, to get to the radial artery. The verdict tended towards mitigating circumstances. Genuine despair, Wolf might've said, leads not to inertia & dreams, but violence. The moral was clear.

❂

We stood before nature like children, & we let our temperaments speak even if it meant inventing when we didn't use nature itself. Like a child standing naked before a hostile crowd, waving his tiny penis. Pissing. Masturbating. Making faces. Daring to be punished. The struggle against the System. A little Oedipus. Longing, not to kill the father & become the father, but to kill the father in such a way as to be at liberty to go on killing him. Again & again.

I can't help thinking of Wolf, playing dead on the beach. How long would he've gone on holding his breath? Or was there a trick? You played dead, as if rehearsing for something you didn't believe could ever be real. Like an actor auditioning for a part in a film. And then the film threatens to come alive. You want to breathe, but you've forgotten how. Or somewhere along the line you determined to forget, saying over & over to yourself:

You don't know where you're going, but your future's already been accessed, the authorities are expecting you.

And just as I'm thinking this a noise comes suddenly from the next room. The sound of someone turning in their bed on the other side of the wall. It only lasts a moment, but in that moment my mood is completely changed. Up till now I'd taken it for granted I was alone. Am I alone?

Two images immediately come to mind. The first is Ascher, watching Wolf act dead. Anxiety clouding his expression. The second is of a man in the public lavatories at the Laboe marina, standing at a urinal, & Ascher, rooted to the spot, staring at the man's enormous prick. The man's bored, faintly sardonic voice:

"What, ain't you ever seen a stiff before, kid?"

The way you might expect James Cagney to say it. Except the man was the Dane.

20
Rapprochement

Louise took a cigarette from her handbag. Tapped it filter-end on her manuscript before lighting it. She drew in deeply. Exhaled. The smoke lingering in the shade of the beach umbrella. *Face it,* she told herself, thrown all of a sudden into a reflex of self-accusation, *you don't know what you want. You don't even know if you enjoyed being fucked last night. You cried because you were angry with yourself. Isn't that it? You felt guilty. Like a child. Because you only want to suffer on your own terms. And what about Adèle? Why'd you ask her to come, when all you do's treat her like a school girl with a crush?*

She finished the cigarette in two long drags & stubbed-out the butt angrily on a stone. she admonished, turning her attention to the manuscript. *You'll wind up luxuriating in despair like Hess,* she thought. *Afraid of being emotionally empty.* She held up the last page on which she'd marked corrections. It belonged to a chapter concerning Derain's arrival in Collioure. During the summer of 1905, Derain's co-conspirator, retired-lawyer Matisse, bearded, hair cropped close to his skull, was dutifully to the village by wife & daughter. Amélie, Marguerite. Derain would have to make do with the company of fishwives. To Maurice de Vlaminck, friend & likewise native of Chatou, he wrote: *The "cunts" here are like fierce wild beasts. When they're tamed you go into their cage, you flatter them, you stroke their backs, but keeping a watchful eye on them. Then, they gobble you up in a single bite.*

This letter was reproduced at the top of the page Luce happened to be holding in her hand. She placed a red mark beside it for further consideration. Derain, a giant of a man, had arrived in Collioure in July, in the middle of the heat, dressed all in white with a red cap on his head. Whatever he thought of the *wild beasts*, he rhapsodised to Vlaminck about the locale: *That country, its people, tanned heads with chrome yellow, mellowed orange skin, blue-black beards... There are women, beautiful gestures, in their black loose blouses, their mantillas... red, green or grey pottery... donkeys, boats, white sails, multicoloured barques. But above all there's the light, a golden blonde light which suppresses shadows & throws me into despair. It's frightening work... Everything I've done till now seems stupid...*

Later: *I try to stop myself between two known shapes. Then it's the utter collapse... You see, everything's upside down. I can feel it. And no-one can show me the right path...*

Louise read mechanically, eyes moving down the page but unable to concentrate. *Cunts. They gobble you up.* Like something Hess'd say. Perhaps he thought about her that way, too. Perhaps they all did. She sighed. Her work was more hopeless than ever. *You want to put in too much. You crowd it, you suffocate it.* The hand holding the page slumped to her lap. *Work*, she thought, *to keep the demons at bay.* But an endless tunnel seemed to be opening before her. Above its mouth, ARBEIT MACHT. But how could she blame Hess for being what he was. Or what she was. *Cunts. You flatter them. You stroke their backs.*

A little distance from the shore Louise spotted him lying on his back, arms at opposed compass points, a human crucifix. And the idea came to her, as if from nowhere, that after all her book was less about Derain, & more about *this*. What was happening to them, to the world. Drifting from one rupture to the next. *Why shouldn't art be just as ruthless & indifferent as life?*

But immediately the thought faltered. How could she ever hope to encompass such a thing in a book? Watching Hess out on the water, she knew her difficulty had as much to do with art mirroring life as it did with pyramids on Mars. She shifted & felt the pain between her legs. Her *cunt*. Where they'd raped her. And in her mind there was no separating them. The way they'd used her like that. Stuffing themselves in her. Bringing to mind the brushstrokes in Derain's paintings. Those savage manual caresses. That unbridled rut. Brutally seizing after the most intimate part of the canvas. To wrench apart the seen world. What an anarchist could've done only by throwing a bomb, Derain did with paint. But the valour of one, against the violation of the other? *Who was it*, she thought, *who said the attainment of pure form is the attainment of life?* A form in *process*. No longer any *thing*, but a fission, a specific energy. Violence without organs. Abstract. Disembodied. Something that might take the place of existence itself. *The scapegoat of all our suffering*. It bored her. Derain bored her. Hess bored her.

She lay the manuscript aside & let her attention wander among the patchwork of beach towels, umbrellas, deckchairs. It was arrested by the spectacle of a woman, about her own age, shimmying awkwardly out of her swimsuit behind a cordon of towels held up by two children. Like the attendant cupids of some Flemish dowager in thrall to her own shame. *A prudish sugar-coated bitch*. The words surprised her.

Immediately she set about rationalising them. Shame, like an interloper in a Rubens. Clinging, in full view of the fleshy indifference of Eden before the Fall, to the rites of respectability. Bodies without history. Naked torsos, exposed groins. The swellings & stirrings underwater. The sky's lactations. *Les lumières très fortes, les ombres très claires*. And the mind's-eye predation, aroused to chromatic frenzies. Rampant blues, yellows, reds. Unbridled. Ubuesque. Fauve. *What that dowager's really ashamed of, is her own indecency. She's just been lying there secretly wanting to be fucked. Right before everyone's eyes!* And not three metres away, two girls embracing in the water. Mouth to mouth. One so drunk she could barely stand. A group of boys played volleyball around them. Louise fingered the gauze of her shawl. Distemper fading to frustrated longing, its cause blatant yet inadmissible. *Why her*

& not you? she thought. *Why you & not her?*

Overhead, a vapour trail dissolved in the sky as though in acid. She shaded her eyes, following the shape of a Mirage jet as it shimmered on the horizon & then also dissolved. A distant rumble sounded in its wake. Dry mechanical thunder. *The reverberations of an emotion that can only be struggled with. Or succumbed to. But which always escapes?* Confronted with the possibility she might never finish writing the book she'd been commissioned to write, she experienced a compensating desire to precipitate some sort of crisis.

"Eluded," she said aloud to herself.

That's what you are. Everything eludes you. Don't you realise you're becoming dead? Like that dowager, with her pointless modesty. *You're not as free as you think you are.* And there was Hess, scowling at her from the water. She tried to ignore him, staring instead at the manuscript in her lap. And at the same time she needed him. To reassure her in his own awkward, abrasive way. His precise sense of others being at fault. And Adèle, what did she suspect? Louise drew her shawl tighter. *Don't be stupid,* she thought. *You'd think it's written all over you...*

But confronted with herself in this way, she could never arrive at the crisis but went directly to the dénouement. Other people were her crisis. They experienced, suffered, had ideas in place of her. For her. Her blood-offerings. Like that placard posted across from the hotel. OFFREZ VOTRE SANG! And always the same question: *Your own or others'?*

21
caméra-stylo

...cinema will gradually break free
from the tyranny of the visual, from
the image for its own sake, from the
immediate & concrete demands of
narrative, to become a means of
writing...
– Alexandre Astruc

When the Wall came down, it was like history itself had ended. Everything was Coca-Cola & fast food escapism. You looked for the aftershock, the delay, the echo, but history would no longer speak to us & be our oracle. With the new decade I enrolled in film school with my auntie's blessing. *Make beautiful things*, she'd said. Beauty in a time of failed euphoria. I'd picked up an old super-8 at one of the junkshops Wolf used to haunt & some cans of discarded film stock. I shot a couple of reels with Ascher in his studio & we spliced the results together with a PDQ Bach soundtrack. The Boatshed Fugue, we dubbed it.

The admissions people must've decided it was okay to let someone like me into their school. But once there, the ideas evaporated. All that time I hadn't realised how everything depended on Ascher. To fill the gap I stole, not bothering to cover my tracks. All property, someone said once, is theft anyway. The whole world was a rerun. A certain contempt was called for. Too shameless & too stupid to admit I'd failed, I rehearsed the usual justifications. The industry was corrupt. It was all about the Deutschmark. No-one appreciated genuine ideas. Everything had already been done. Critics were slaves to the marketplace. Film was just TV by other means, wanting only to be saleable more, more accessible, more apologetic.

It was easy to peddle a contrary line. Our dead fathers bequeathed a useless optimism in exhausted ideals. The whole planet was going to hell. East & West didn't matter. Suddenly we had to invent our own meanings. Whatever chances there were of exhausting its stock of melodrama, the odds were stacked against us inventing new ones. The lost & imperilled turned for guidance to the oraculating idiot box. That squared anus of the airwaves. If all else failed, you could still take the crap prime time threw at you & hurl it right back.

Of course I wanted someone to blame. What else are fathers for? Too bad I didn't know who mine was. If he'd stuck around, maybe he could've shouldered his share of the mess we were in. People said I was lucky. Like Jesus Christ, only without the downside. But by the time the Wall came down, it was too late. There was no getting away from that absence. Unable to suspend disbelief in my own existence, life itself grew inauthentic. I hid in theatres, watching shadows on a screen, like a private confessional. The confessor indifferent to whether I came or went.

Bored with school I left & moved to Prague, head full of the cinematic revolution I was planning to orchestrate. Arriving at the main station was like stepping back in history. A crashed time machine where past & future could as easily be exchanged as suspended. The escapist in me found a natural refuge there. Like one of Herzog's dwarves. If it was possible to imagine a time before cinema, Prague might've been it.

There were no intermissions & the show went on non-stop. I bought a notebook. I thought all I had to do was write down everything I saw. I made films in my head that I straightaway forgot. Onto the next scene. Someone gave me a job on the set of a film about a complicated assassination plot. It involving two octogenarians, a man & woman, out to blow up Konrad Adenauer. Everyone died in the end, except Adenauer. It was very poignant. I worked my way up to being someone's assistant. All the films were about death. They were stories dead people told themselves to keep up the pretence of being alive. I drank. The more I drank, the more I convinced myself the only authentic stance was a blanket refusal. The world was corrupt. Cinema was corrupt. For the price of a bottle, I could've even told you how & why. All I was waiting for was the big offer, so I could tell them where they could shove it.

The big offer! One day I woke up with my entire existence amputated. What'd happened to that little cinema at Laboe? Where we used to hang out all those years before, watching Claudia Cardinale & Klaus Kinski on a doomed riverboat, while Rolf screwed his girls & the smell of grilled *dorade* wafted through the door? I discovered my very own lost childhood to mourn. I sensed the form of a film I was living but couldn't grasp. A form of survival-after-death which goes on only as long as you can bear to watch. It didn't occur to me that stories themselves were only useful if they got you to a place you need to go. Or helped make sense of the journey.

✺

Then one day, out of the blue, Wolf.

It was September, 1994. The Cairo Eugenics Conference buzzing in the news. I'd managed to scrape by, ghosting treatments & the odd film review for the *Prager Zeitung*. I'd just escaped a five-hour screening of pre-Wall propaganda footage, part of some festival or other. It was a Sunday. Purely by chance I was parked in a grungy underground bar called the Zed Klub. A black-light dive you entered down a stairway between a strip joint & a slot machine parlour. The deejay was making noise for a non-existent clientele. With a tray of two-for-one vodkas, I was slowly getting the upper hand over another day's sense of achievement.

Then it was like someone toggled the reality switch. Cue to a scene in a bar: the stranger you recognise from ten years ago, appearing out of nowhere. Drinks. All that crap. The sort of scene you'd despise yourself for ever writing. Well that's how it was. Wolf just coming up & asking for a light, like a regular come-on. He was wearing a red T-shirt that said *Chaos Reigns*. Grey suit jacket & jeans over Ferragamo cowboy boots. He looked like he'd slept in them. His hair was down around his shoulders. At first it didn't twig, who he was. It'd been so long. But he picked me straight off. *Haven't changed a bit*. Whatever. We had those drinks. Reminisced. Shot the shit.

Wolf filled me in on the success story he'd made of himself. Finished school. Took classes in political economy in Frankfurt. Mathematics & Planning. Psychology. This & that. Won a post-grad scholarship in philosophy. Freiberg. Dropped out. Universities, he proclaimed, were the dustbins of the failing middle class. He'd had some run-ins with the *authorities*. Said he was working out a manifesto for our disillusioned times. A repudiation of something called the *New Ethics*. A lot of crap about sustainability, race science, Malthus. The next battleground in the struggle against the neo-fascists.

That was five years after reunification & everything was still going wrong. Different brands of ultrism on the rise left, right & centre. Holocaust denial. Ethnic cleansing. Secret sterilisation programmes. The further east you went, the more *ultra* it got. Names like Eugen Fischer & Ernst Rüden were turning up in serious discussion about EU immigration policy. Skinheads paraded openly in Prague. Slovakia, Austria, Hungary, Romania, all installed rightwing gimps to run the government. Yugoslavia was ritually suiciding itself while the UN stood by & watched fascist death squads rape & execute with impunity. Wolf was on his way down there. Sarajevo. Searching for who the fuck knows what. The authentic history of our times, maybe.

❂

Can you honestly tell me, hand on shoulder, giving me one of those looks, *that you've ever written one true sentence?* Wolf used the interrogative form, but with purely rhetorical intent. It was just before he went south. Taking me to task for my lack of commitment. As far as I could see, truth didn't enter into it. Every standpoint was in some essential sense *equally the case.* Equally *true.* The whole circus of human aspiration. Frailty. Stupidity. Love & hate. X-rated. *Without any clear-cut moral standpoint.* A film either worked or it didn't. Well...

To Wolf, nothing at all was innocent. Nothing uncompromised, unimplicated. Had it ever been otherwise? The question wasn't *what the truth was supposed to be*, but *who had the moral competence to decide?* As far as I could see, cinema was a divided objectivity. Simply believing in right-mindedness wasn't good enough. It never had been. For cinema to exist, it could only be born of disillusionment. Amen.

By the time he came back, Wolf had aged considerably. He looked like Jack Palance in *Bagdad Café.* Or the way Palance looked in all his films. He never spoke about what happened in Bosnia. But there was something in his eyes. Like a fanatic in the onset of a crisis of belief. Who'd do anything to smother his own doubt.

22
Anchoïade

In her broad-brimmed sun hat, Luce reminded of that painting of Madame Matisse, green shadows obliterating her face. A halo of blue filtered through the umbrella, like light through a piece of abraded glass. She'd tied on a linen wrap, the pale green shawl loosely covering her shoulders. Hess sat up. There was a dull pain behind his eye. He turned to say something & saw Luce's face twisting around above him, so comically it made him laugh. But there was nothing funny in her expression. She was saying... But he couldn't understand what she was saying. Dizzy. Then his head cleared. He remembered, she'd made a reservation at a restaurant for noon. He could see the hands on the church clock poised to overlap.

While Luce gathered her manuscript, Hess slipped out of his swimming shorts into a pair of white chinos & India cotton shirt. As he was dressing, he noticed the girl in the red bikini scrutinising him. He fingered the buttons at his crotch to gauge her reaction. She yawned & turned over onto her back. Hess stood there with his shadow falling across the girl's face. He toyed with the idea of some alter-ego of his reaching across to slide the fabric of her bikini away from her breasts. Circle a brown nipple with his tongue, etcetera. The girl lowered a pair of Italian sunglasses over her eyes & seemed to go to sleep.

Idiot, he told himself. A moment later he & Luce were threading their way down the strand. Hess, as always, impatient with the crowd, the unconscious fleshy meandering. Eventually they arrived at a courtyard restaurant off the rue Colbert. Three tables hidden behind a trellis with vines. The sunlight was so bright it bleached the shadows.

"It makes me sick," Hess complained. "People everywhere. The place's crawling with them…"

"You never cared before."

Rather than argue, he focused on the lunch menu. *Une nouvelle vague se répand à Collioure: après le Fauvisme… l'Anxovinisme!*

"For Christ's sake."

Bombas au bacalao, sauce aux anchois 8€, Cannelonis au veau et anchois de Collioure 8€, Fideau aux anchois frais et salés 8€, Seiches aux pignons, raisins et anchois 8€50, Salade de fenouil et anchois 7€, Tapenade maison aux anchois 6€, Poisson mariné aux anchois 8€.

"All they have's bloody anchovies."

"Try turning the page."

Hess flipped the menu. *Pois chiches au cumin 4€, Salade de lentilles et pancetta ibérique 4€, Caviar d'aubergines au piment d'Espelette 6€, Houmous de pois chiches 5€, Salade de petits poulpes 7€, Escalivada de poivrons rouges 6€50, Escalivada gitana 6€50, Patatas à l'allioli 5€50, Poulpe à la galicienne 8€50, Brandade de morue gratinée 7€50, Coustellou rôti au mile 7€, Boles de picoulat 7€50, Poulet frit à l'ail 7€50, Petites patates grenailles rôties et allioli 5€50, Calamars à l'encre 7€50, Escargots à la catalane 7€50, Joues de porc au Banyuls 8€, Chorizo au cidre 4€.*

"You don't seriously intend to eat any of this, do you?"

Luce hummed while scanning the page in front of her. A waiter appeared with a basket of bread, a bowl of tapenade, a carafe of iced water. At the two other tables, parties of four sat huddled close over their fish. Watching them made Hess nauseous. *The sea & its alleged miracles.* His mouth was parched, he'd had nothing to drink since morning. Luce, meanwhile, gave her order to the waiter. The man leant down as if he was hard of hearing.

"Vin rosé," Hess tried not to shout at him. "Make it a bottle."

The waiter grimaced, expectant. Hess stared till he went away, then turned his attention back to Luce. She was gazing past him at some hanging gardenia with a faraway look that made him feel as if he didn't exist.

"Where's Ada?" he asked in a flat, uninterested voice.

"She says she's had enough of you for one day…"

"D'you think she can manage on her little lonesome?" he asked, watching Luce dip a crust of bread in the tapenade.

"She isn't a child you know," she said.

Hess regarded her sceptically.

"Why'd you invite her? We hardly see each other as it is."

"Hess," she replied, in a tired voice. "It never worked when we did."

"At least this way, I suppose, we both still have something to look forward to. What *I* have to look forward to, I really couldn't say. But when I was a boy my auntie always told me to keep an open mind."

"She must've been a sensible woman, your aunt."

"A shame you never got to meet her."

"Is she dead?"

"Not exactly. She communes with figments."

"Well, if it makes her happy."

"What it makes her is mentally ill."

"Don't get worked up, Hess."

"Not *worked up*. Merely *clarifying*."

"Well, at least it's cooler here. Usually," Luce said, "I can't eat when it's hot. I think I'll try the Anchoïade. How about you?"

Hess grunted: "Eating spoils my appetite."

"Or the grilled sardines. Or mussels marinated in Banyuls, cooked over vine wood. A local speciality, it says. Sound tempting? Maybe that's what I'll get. Sure you won't…?"

When the waiter returned – *what the hell* – Hess ordered some salted nuts. He wasn't sure what kind. And – just to keep on the safe side – another bottle of rosé.

✦

Hess'd already finished the first bottle by the time the waiter returned with the second. Pouring the wine he suddenly said:

"D'you ever get the feeling we're only here to kill time, yet already failing? It's time after all that kills us. It's just a matter of waiting our turn."

Luce stared at him a moment then thought better of replying. The waiter reappeared, carrying a tray with the assortment of dishes Luce had ordered. A silence settled over the table as she ate. Hess quickly finished his glass & poured another. He resolutely said nothing. While Luce ate her mussels, or sardines, or whatever the hell they were, the memory of his breakfast conversation with Ada came back to him. Only distorted now. Caricatured. Like a situation in a film. Two people sitting at a table, a man & a woman. He toyed with variations on that theme. It'd be easy, after all, to construct an entire narrative simply around the as-yet-undisclosed drama of those two people, any two people, sitting at a table:

Who are they? How'd they get there? What's their relation to one another? Suddenly they're about to leave. Two empty glasses on a soiled tablecloth. The woman hands the man some money under the table, so he can pay without being ashamed. He gets angry. Something's said, voices are raised. "I'm not such a slave as I was." Does he really say that? Or else the story proceeds without ever developing. Events simply follow one another without cause or meaningful effect. Just as they do in reality.

✦

Hess ordered a third bottle, producing an indistinct grunt from the waiter. The waiter took his time clearing away the empty plates. Once he'd finished, Luce leant forward with her arms folded in front of her on the yellow tablecloth, shawl draping her shoulders. She remained silent for some time, gazing at the empty glass as she rotated it between her fingers.

"Shouldn't we talk?" Hess prompted.

Luce looked up. He could see himself in her eyes come gradually into focus.

"Should we?" she said.

"You seem to be far away."

Luce shook her head: "It's nothing."

Hess regarded her sceptically then poured some wine into her glass. The gesture took her off guard. She gave the wine an apprehensive look. Hess set the bottle down & spoke while considering the contents of his own glass. Or perhaps the reflection in the bottom of it. Or the smear of fingerprints around the rim. Who could say?

"When I woke up this morning I couldn't remember who I was." He checked to see Luce was listening & continued: "At first, everything was simply blank. But then the blankness expanded into every part of the room. I began to panic. Hyperventilate. I thought something was taking over my awareness, doing away with me, bit by bit. It was just an anxiety attack. Nothing happened."

Luce drank off the contents of her glass & held it out for Hess to refill. Her gaze was firmly riveted to a point below his left shoulder. As soon as he'd put the bottle back down she emptied her glass & held it out to him again.

"Are you sure everything's alright?" Hess asked.

"Perfectly," she said.

He poured again. *It might be amusing*, he thought, *to watch her get drunk*. At least then the odds would be evened out.

"Anything else?" he asked.

"No," she said. "Everything's fine the way it is."

"Well anyway," he began, picking at a piece of crust that lay on the tablecloth. "I went to your room. You weren't there. Ada asked if we'd been together. So I guessed something was the matter…"

"I told you, it's nothing."

"Funny thing is, I had this dream. You'll think it's strange, because darling Ada was in it. Remember the last time we came here, how we got stuck at Béziers because of a fire on the tracks? Well, that was it. Ada was waiting on the platform beside me, & on the opposite platform were all these other people. Except they were really us. Like there was a giant mirror down the middle of the tracks & we were watching our reflections. Except Ada wasn't in it. Her reflection was missing. She was frantic. Going back & forth along the platform trying to find where they'd hidden it. Then all of a sudden she was running down the tracks & the train, with all those reflections looking out the windows, was chasing her."

Hess paused to take a sip of wine. While he'd been speaking, he'd broken the crust into tiny pieces which now littered the tablecloth in front of him.

"D'you remember where the train cuts out past the lagoon? Well all of a sudden I was there. I was walking along a dyke, the sea on one side & the lagoon on the other. The grass all along the tracks had been burned & was still smouldering. The air was acrid. I can't remember what happened then. I was alone. The sky was grey. It was low tide. The sea was far off, across a tidal flat. Stones seemed to pile up everywhere. Then I saw a crowd was gathered in a circle below the dyke. They were the reflections from Béziers, except now Ada was there too. She looked at me, then looked down at something on the ground. A child was lying there in the middle of the circle. Where the child's face should've been was a jellyfish with its tentacles hanging down." He swept the breadcrumbs off the tablecloth. "Of course, you know who the child was supposed to be, don't you?"

157

"Who?" Luce asked, clutching her glass in both hands.

"Maybe we should go," Hess suggested.

"No," she said. "I want to finish my wine. Who was the child?"

"Don't they say everyone in your dreams is really yourself?"

"And Adèle? Was she you in your dream too?"

Hess laughed. Luce drained her glass & poured another.

"D'you remember Reinaldo Arenas?" he asked.

Luce shook her head.

"He was a Cuban writer. He committed suicide in New York, where he was dying of AIDS. Before he killed himself, he wrote that an exile is a person who, having lost a loved one, keeps searching for the face he loves in every new face. And forever deceiving himself, thinks he's found it."

"Well he wouldn't've written it after he killed himself, would he?" Luce met his gaze, a hardness around her eyes. "Besides, exile can mean all sorts of things. It can mean…"

"It's just the image that occurred to me," Hess interrupted weakly. "It doesn't mean anything."

23
kraftwerk

...the photograph allows us on the one hand to admire in reproduction something our eyes alone couldn't have taught us to love, & on the other, to admire the painting as a thing in itself whose relation to something in nature has ceased to be the justification of its existence.
– André Bazin

The old Kaspar Hauser character at the Oldenberg record shop had no clue what he was ordering, just stocked anything "new" on account of the vacation crowd, with a little judicious prompting in the right areas. Everything else in the shop, if it wasn't Mozart or Krautrock, was strictly *heimat*. We'd cruise over there each Friday afternoon while beach-goers filled-out the aisles on their way back to the campsites & bungalows. Wolf would fire requests at Kasper Hauser while Ascher & I took turns in the sound booth, pretending to be interested in Burt Baccarach or some Beach Boys tribute. Marita, meanwhile, would elbow her way alphabetically through the drawers, slipping all the best discs under her tie-dyed blouse but leaving the top buttons undone.

While Hauser was busy playing DJ, she'd toy with the jerk at the cash register, asking could he order this record or that record. Letting him get an eyeful of young-girl breasts, never guessing what was going on right under his nose. We fancied ourselves the only kids in all Schleswig-Holstein who'd even heard of modern music. All thanks to Wolf who besides war memorabilia & agitprop productively spent his Aachen years hoarding obscure fanzines & bootleg cassettes. Mail-ordered at his relatives' expense from all points north, south, east & west.

When Wolf left, Ascher became inward, spending most of his time drawing. And when he wasn't drawing, he'd sulk with Marita. She started pimping herself on the Strandweg, sitting on the wall in a bikini waving her legs at all the family men passing by. With the money she rented a derelict boathouse for a hangout. She told Ascher it should be his studio, like she believed in him. We set it up with coloured lights, a turntable & junkyard car seats. From constant playing we wore out the vinyl on our favourite tracks. *Venus in Furs* with John Cale's crazy viola. New York Dolls *Dance like a Monkey*. The Vibrators. Early Stooges retard-bop. Joe Strummer *I'm so bored with the USA*...

Ascher's working method was to nail whole sheets of sailcloth or ratty tarpaulin to the walls & cover them with industrial acrylic & spray-paint filched from the dry docks. Pieces of newsprint. Torn posters. Ticket stubs. Stencils. Cardboard signs. Flattened packing boxes. Street litter. Any kind of junk. A convulsive palimpsest of force-feedback proto-punk & machine aesthetic, like a threesome with Kurt Schwitters, Iggy Pop & Kraftwerk. Forces of weird subterranean chaos spiralled into infinite depths, returning transfigured to the surface.

He composed intuitively, layering & gouging to produce weird archaeological forms. Half cave painting, half urban graffiti. The same motifs recurred. Swirling eyes & suns. Lending coherence to what might've seemed random. But he didn't figure on showing his work to anyone. His attempts had always met with derision at home & at school. To escape his brother, he constructed a loft with a mattress & moved into the boatshed on a permanent basis. And he quit school. We faked a letter saying he'd moved to Aachen, like Wolf had. No-one from the *Jugendamt* bothered him, so maybe it worked.

161

The boathouse floor got to be like an archaeological site, crusted with paint & garbage. Things just accumulated. He flung paint working barefoot, the soles of his feet tracking weird calligraphies on whatever lay in his path. His hair & clothes were a mess. It was wasted effort persuading Ascher to be more ambitious about his art. The way people used *ambitious* to mean suits & ties. TV celebs. Investment bankers. Big-note critics. Fancy cocktails with little canapés on toothpicks. What it should've meant was *serious*. The rest was for clowns. Serious was for revolutionaries. Fuck the canapés.

Compared to the prints my auntie had hanging all around her house, Ascher's paintings looked like the work of a cannibal. He was as far ahead of his time as a Neanderthal was of the twentyfirst century. Marita's idea of taking on the world was we'd roll up the smaller paintings, strap them to our backs, & bike into Kiel to pitch them to galleries. But it'd take even an idiot five seconds to see they only displayed junk, so we figured we'd have to train it to Hamburg instead. You could do it without a ticket no problem.

We'd get there in the morning & footslog round the city with a phone directory till closing time, hitting as many galleries as we could. After, we'd sit on a curb & watch the hustlers on the prowl up & down the Reeperbahn. After the third go round, the gallery assistants copped to the act. We were these punks trying to flog shit a monkey had crapped on a canvas, or whatever. Some joker had probably told us it was art. They'd laugh, say *Hang in there, kid, maybe monkey shit'll be really big some day.* In another time & place, Ascher might've been a genius. Some '80s primitive child. Instead all he got was the long finger.

You could see it going on like that. Not a chance in hell those galleries were ever going to take his stuff. Dumb even to've tried. It must've been funny as hell to someone. They just strung him along with condescending bullshit till all concerned got bored

162

with it or they plain shoved us out the door. It lasted till the end of summer, when the jerks in their Brooks Brothers suits found better things to do with their time. I felt embarrassed for Ascher & then embarrassed by him. His neediness, his humiliation. Well who needs enemies, eh? Marita egged him on, taking secret pleasure in his torment. The more he suffered, the more she drove him to suffer. And the more she drove him, the more feverishly he painted. It was like watching a person who can't swim, out over their head, clutching at those who instead of trying to save him are intent on watching him drown.

Probably Marita understood him better than I ever could. As soon as she was legal, they got hitched. A civil job in Hamburg. The witnesses where strangers who happened to be in the waiting room. I was too young to sign. Stuck in that limbo of the sub-proletariat, cretinised by society. You serve out your sentence till deemed fit to join the ranks of the great unwashed. They say it's because people live longer nowadays. Or take longer dying. So it's only natural, isn't it, to have to wait in line. Besides, infantilism makes for a better quality of citizen. In the race towards mediocrity, it's hard not to be a winner.

But why Ascher married her, I couldn't say. Like a man wanting to cut his own balls off out of spite. It was the beginning of the end. Maybe it'd always been the beginning of the end. Maybe there was no end. He developed the disease where he couldn't live outside his asylum. A sucker's disease. But we were all suckers. Never able to forgive ourselves for who we were. The irretrievable, inexcusable loss of everything we might've loved, if we'd had the chance. The System likes to teach you to be wasteful in consumption, but efficient in everything else. Efficient in imagination, in reproduction, in death. Maybe that's what made Ascher's suicide so vicious, more than it had to be. Spurred by an inner need the world had no place for.

He never admitted knowing what Marita did behind his back.

163

Working shifts at the docks while she stayed home screwing up a storm. The Dane regularly came through town & slapped her around a bit, the way she liked it rough sometimes. Gave as good as she got. Fed off the pain. Made everyone around her hungry for it. She was Ascher's cruel muse. Elusive, mocking, insistent, available. He'd bury his head in the sand & only stop to ask how deep to make the hole. It was like he'd become that part of himself he'd tried to cut out of his skin & smear on canvas. The narcissistic wound that never heals.

Like an idiot, I envied him. His private hell. His martyrdom. I went alone to cinemas & watched the same films over & over again, absorbing the lives of others, trying to divine the secret of the tortured soul. But my conscience would never be pure. Staring into the screen the way a man stares at a mirror. To discover himself. And a face, like Eddie Constantine's, staring back. Saying *film consists of twentyfour lies per second...*

24
Frames

Luce was in a complex mood when they left the restaurant. Proceeding along rue Pasteur towards the market, they stopped at a bookstand, where Hess found a second-hand copy of *Bouvard et Pécuchet*. Luce restlessly flipped through old magazines, twisting & untwisting the strap of her shoulder-bag. She looked unhappy. Hess, unready to acknowledge the day might already have ended in defeat, suggested they take a bottle up to her room.

"Let's just go back to the hotel & fuck."

Luce yawned.

"I can't," she said. "And you're lousy when you're drunk anyway."

Hess stared at her incredulously.

"Said the princess to the pea. Have you looked at yourself lately?"

"Besides, you were always lousy when I was drunk, too."

"Is that your idea of a joke?"

"No, Hess, you're very far from my idea of a joke," dropping the magazine back onto the pile she'd taken it from. "Or I just don't have any humour left. Or I've got a nasty imagination & want to be alone with it. Or I don't feel well. Take your pick."

"If I hadn't sat on a damned train for thirtysix hours to come here, you'd still feel the same, is that it?"

Hess gritted his teeth. He knew what Luce really intended was to see Ada. The idea riled him. He felt his temper rise, irrationally supposing a kind of conspiracy by increments. That everything was slipping between his fingers, even this. He gripped Luce's arm & she winced. The shawl fell away from her shoulders & Hess saw the bruises on her arms. A sudden imploring expression came into her eyes & Hess let go of her. He watched his hand fall, without understanding the intention behind his own gesture.

Luce drew the shawl back around her shoulders & walked off. Hess, immobile, lost sight of her in the crowd. He tried to make sense of what'd just happened but couldn't. *You're pathetic*, he told himself, aware he was beginning to attract the attention of passers-by. Then he swung about & pushed along the busy street, not caring where he was headed.

Somehow he managed to wind right back around to Port d'Avall. He came to an intersection across from a pharmacist's. He dug in his pockets for his prescription. The air inside was cool at least. Cool & antiseptic. Hess eyed the pharmacist's white uniform while she glanced over his script, then disappeared behind a partition. Moments later, clutching his Flaubert & a box of sumatriptan, Hess stepped back out onto the pavement & was immediately overwhelmed by the heat. He found a tapas bar half a block away. The barman saluted as he came in. Hess recognised him. It was the same place he'd wound up with the three Argentinians the night before. He returned the greeting & asked for a carafe of Roussillon.

"Bravo!" the barman grinned.

Hess didn't feel overly triumphant as he tipped back the first glass of red wine. But he did feel his body relaxing into a general sullenness that was at least an improvement. His reflection ogled him from the window. A constant stream of traffic blocked all view of the sea. Slipping three pills into his mouth he washed them down with a second glass. Bouvard & Pécuchet sneered up at him from the table. He felt the wine slosh around in his guts. The book cover showed two dogs in top hats, breeches & tailcoats, standing on hind legs outside a parlour window. Hess belched from the corner of his mouth. One of the dogs was leaning on an umbrella, the crook of its handle gripped in yellow kid-skin gloves, while gazing intently through the window at a young chamber maid. The voyeur's companion, meanwhile, was busy pissing against a wall. Hess tentatively raised the cover of the book with his left index finger to read the first line. *Comme il faisait une chaleur de 33 degrés, le boulevard Bourdon se trouvait absolument désert...*

Except that outside it was well over thirtythree & the street wasn't deserted. He leant back in his chair, taking another mouthful. Just then a female gendarme passed by the window. Brunette. Reflexively his eyes followed her blue-clad arse till it disappeared among the traffic. *L'air sérieux de cet cul me frappe,* he intoned in cod-Flaubert, *mais son aspect aussi aimable me charme de suite.* Sucking air between his teeth, the idea of that cop's arse struck him as an obscenity. With a kind of sluttish insouciance, how everything symbolised in that uniform suddenly implied its opposite, its illicit counterpart. The stilettos of a streetwalker who feels through your pockets. The streetlamp an underage hustler pouts beneath. Brothel-creepers in doorways. The hand wielding a truncheon & the body passively receiving its blows.

He saw again the accusation in Luce's eyes as she'd turned away from him in the street. The bruises on her arms. What they aroused in him. An image of a hotel room. Luce's body in the stifling heat, against the white bed sheets. Febrile. Naked. Awaiting the infliction of desire. He saw, very close up, her swollen lips. Parted. Murmuring. Or perhaps laughing. And that laughter turning to something vicious, dominated by the violence of frustrated actions. Unconsummated scenes of bloodlust. A petrified fly-on-the-wall. Ada twisting in her hands a swollen voodoo homunculus, slicked with spit, working it inside her. Clockwise, anticlockwise. One thrust after another. And all the while Luce fixing him with that look, like Caravaggio's *Medusa.*

168

The scene ran on. Looping. Repeating. A pornographic Möbius strip of rough tongues & unyielding mouths. Drunken, anaesthetised copulations in strange rooms. Stairwells. Arcades. In the shadows of crowded streets. Laughter again. And suddenly his own mouth, fitted in place of Luce's cunt. While Ada, dildo rearing its enormous head between her thighs, proceeded to fuck him.

❂

Hess stared at the now empty carafe. *Like an intestine's peristalsis*, he muttered. Flashback to the journey from Prague. The horror. Like a B-film from which, for thirtysix hours, there'd been no escape. A nice symbolic opening for the masochist stripped bare before his own impotence, tied to a chair in that mind's-eye cinema, watching himself being sodomised on a giant screen. *Well it's no secret*, Hess thought. The look of distaste on Luce's face. Thinking of the last time they'd made love. Her unreactive body. How she seemed to want to make him as aware as possible of just how much she suffered. Like some grossly amplified, inert thing his own body had attached itself to.

Reminding of how they'd first met, in the offices of the *Prager Zeitung*. Luce was researching an article on the paedophile artist, Egon Schiele, whose paintings had been looted by the Nazis during the war. She'd just interviewed one of the curators from the Jewish Museum, who was suing to have them returned. How during that first encounter she'd naturally assumed he was homosexual. Yet a week later there she was, openly seducing him at the Riviera Club on Národní Street. Hess glanced at his watch. Twenty-past-six. *Time to move onto the next scene.*

"L'addition," he told the waiter & paid.

For a while Hess stood on the terrace overlooking Plage d'Avall, contemplating the scene. The beautiful people were sipping cocktails on the decks of the yachts. Rewind one hundred years: *Boats at Collioure*, 1905. Seen through a filter of Mourvedre, Carignan, Grenache, Cinsault. Glopping from a broken fisheye lens. Just as Derain, after one of his orgies. Unrepentant in red & green. A blue-black sail. A raw band of sky. Some secret chemical that fuelled the mind's panopticon like an aphrodisiac. Only the chemical had run out, the artist depleted of his vision. Washed-up. A name pencilled in the margins. What'd it matter if he was a genius, a fool, or simply a man who'd seen the world with his own eyes in all its naked derangement?

A pair of children with plastic buckets were wading among the rock pools, collecting stones. Hess watched them. Perhaps everything humanity hoped for could be summed up right there. One specific of a general condition. Sort stones on a beach. What was Derain to the encroaching mania for categorisation? Order for the sake of order. To stave off entropy. A hundred years, or a thousand, or ten thousand. When the sea will've moved on. Pursued by a desert.

A set of steps led down to the promenade. At the end of which, the Marina. And beyond that, Plage Boramar with the sun slanting upon it now from behind the Miradou. The umbrellas had all been put away. Already the strand was in shadow. A faint breeze crept up from the water. The Modigliani woman was still there. Hair hanging damp around her shoulders, the open volume of Bulgakov resting between her breasts. Even with her hair that way she reminded him of Jeanne Hébuterne. Those eyes. The unnaturally long neck, like an invitation to violence. Hess gave up watching her & crossed the footbridge, joining the crowd on the strand.

Modigliani had died of tuberculosis. A slow & miserable death, in a pauper's ward. He was thirtysix. Hébuterne committed suicide the next day. Pregnant with their child.

25
entropy

Lying on your back, on a bed, in a room. Sunlight between Venetian blinds. Seven-fortysix a.m. You dreamt you were woken by something breaking. A sound from the street, through the open window. But it was only a radio. Or a car. Noises that approach as if from afar, then fade. You stood up & went to look outside. The car park below was deserted. After a while, three boys appeared from the right, dressed in black. They crossed the car park silently, as if going to a funeral. One of them carried his jacket over his right arm. Above, the sky was grey, leaden. When you looked again, the boys were gone. A church bell rang. Ten minutes too soon. Ten minutes for all eternity. You went back to bed & lay down, arms folded over your chest, unconsciously arranging yourself the way a corpse is arranged.

In Wolf's philosophy, everyone always has a choice. Because choice implies responsibility. And responsibility gives you someone to blame. After the fire, their old beach house was torn down to make way for a supermarket. He never forgave his mother for what she'd done. And yet every other summer he'd come back to lay a wreath in the supermarket car park. In

172

memory of a lost childhood.

Ascher never came back. What was there to come back to? He wanted to know what distinguishes a human being from a jellyfish, something whose existence is nothing but a type of palpitation. Who knows if he found an answer. He didn't have far to look. A human's a complex of sentimentality & spite. What more did it take for us all to betray each other in the end? Ineptitude? Stupidity? Carelessness? Fear? Fear of our vulnerabilities. Why call it betrayal? It wasn't always like that. Wolf & I. Ascher. Blood brothers. Perhaps we never really parted but only diverged. Like mirrors that reflect one another. And that spot where the mirrors become blind. Where precisely nothing at all's visible. And now, in a few hours, we'll lay Ascher to rest. His memory. Or whatever you want to call it.

From the beginning I made coming back a non-option. I telephoned, less & less, months stretching to years. The sense of an obligation harder & harder to meet. The tiredness creeping into my auntie's voice, like she'd held on all those years & now was letting go. And then they sent her to a rest home & it was like talking to a stranger. How'd it happen so fast? She was young, she grew old in the blink of an eye. I couldn't bear it. Too full of myself to see how she suffered in her loneliness. Suffering that could never be undone. And Marita, who I sent a bottle of cheap perfume as a birthday gift. Erasing her body from memory as soon as the ink on the letter had dried. Embarked on that great romance of repudiation & denial. And it dawning by degrees, how this was all my life was ever going to be.

Ascher's death embarrasses me.

It was on one of his pilgrimages that Wolf called to let me know he'd found Ascher living in Hamburg. Goethestraße. Near the Altona Bahnhof. He was scraping by. Marita had taken off with the kids, to be with her mother in Copenhagen. Their marriage was a disaster from the start. In all probability, the kids weren't even his. The picture Wolf painted was of a man drowning in a river of burnt bridges & being washed out to sea. His attic was full of crazy half-finished pictures five metres high. *Cave paintings in a room above a city*, Wolf said. He'd sunk into himself, bled onto the walls, drank like a bum to quiet his demon. He beckoned the disaster on. It'd be his masterpiece.

For once Wolf's philosophy failed him. People think an artist, encumbered with all the attitudes of past & present, has a duty to ask himself: *How do I separate myself from all this? What am I trying to achieve?* But what if an artist's like a child, who looks at the world & asks: *What do they want from me?* & does the precise opposite? A child who doesn't examine its motives but simply acts, out of a perverse compulsion, without having any choice.

Ascher used to say all his thoughts were wound up like a coil in his head, & only when by painting could he feel them slowly unwind. Till he'd come to a stop before the picture in front of him & everything became clear. And that's how he'd know it was finished. His life was the same. Attempting to reverse an inward spiral, he'd found it as hopeless as reversing entropy. Like a child in a sandpit, running in circles. Black sand & white sand churned to grey. And no matter how long or how fast he runs in the opposite direction, never able to undo the process. To separate again the white sand from the black.

Before she walked out on him, Marita filled Ascher in on the whole story. Laid it all out. Every filthy last detail. As if all those years had been nothing but an expression of the low opinion she had of herself. And the lower opinion he had of himself. Everything wasted, dried up, shrivelled into nothing. But who am I to judge. Ascher refused to believe it was the end. Like that wasn't enough & he had to have more. Like the humiliation was the only thing letting him breathe. Marita got a court order. To keep him away from the kids. She said he freaked them out. As if she was a paragon of all virtue & sanity. He got sore about the kids. Ascher the devoted family man: I can't see it somehow. Maybe it was because of what he'd gone through, wanting to spare them all that. To be there. Who knows what he thought.

But it got to him. Messed with whatever sanity he had left. Already a wreck, he became a ghost. Wolf somehow kept track of him. Hamburg. Copenhagen. Kiel. There was a whole string of phone numbers I was supposed to call, but never did. Wolf tried to smooth things over, sent money, put some sort of guilt-trip on Marita. Did he think he was doing Ascher any favours? Maybe he had something on his own conscience. Maybe he'd been screwing Marita, too, on the side, like everything else he did on the side. Persuaded her to hold-off on a divorce. Why? I don't know. I didn't ask her & she didn't say.

Was that why Ascher waited so long to do himself in? The final straw? Believing there was only one future & he'd blown it?

❂

Perhaps you knew all along that insincerity's also the mask of a deeper evasion. The fear of an abyss inside ordinary things. The abyss behind the eyes. Under the bed. Beneath your feet. Like a child's inadmissible nightmare. Should a man be punished merely for being insincere? And what should his punishment be? To stand naked & confess? Self-accuse? Confess? Recant? Make himself as grotesque as possible? But you did nothing. Others perhaps. It was always the others. Who did the things you didn't dare to do. What you didn't dare even to think. Them not you. You barely even existed. They made you up. As a kind of alibi. And now you've got to go on bearing the consequences. Who were they? The boy lying on the sand who killed his mother? The boy who cried wolf? Erupting into flame the way the rising & setting sun erupts on water...?

26
Cordon Sanitaire

The sun began going down by increments. Shadows falling across the façades of the houses the way stillness settles over an audience in a theatre. The pain in her arm throbbed where Hess had taken hold of her. She knew Adèle would be waiting for her, wanting to be placated. The thought made her suddenly more fatigued than she already was. And yet, at the same time, conscious of an arousal formed of disavowal. An arousal tinged with disgust. At herself. Hess. The pointlessness. At everything. *No. It's not as bad as all that*, she thought. *You'll survive.*

She stood across the street from the hotel, staring at the window display of a wine shop. In its reflection she could see the balcony of her room & the shuttered window facing onto it. Inside it'd be dark. She'd be able to lie there in the darkness & not have to think. But even as she thought this, a conversation without interlocutors was rehearsing itself in her head: *You can see objects, but not what people are like… Absence & practiced avoidance… Whispering in the secrecy of your own four walls… Somewhere you can't be found…Too tired for this…* The voices circled without ever communicating. Like flies in the middle of a room. Strange triangulations that only approximated a closed circle. Forever disjoined. Erratic. Reminding her of the way Hess retreated into paradox whenever he sensed he was being threatened. Or whether he sensed it or not. A reflex. Not to be pinned down to a single meaning.

Inside the wine shop a woman in a black dress was watching her from behind a counter. Their eyes met & Louise blushed. The woman signalled towards the door but Louise shook her head & turned away. A steady stream of traffic in both directions forced her to wait to cross the street. The Triumph sat there baking in the sun in front of the boulangerie. She remembered what she'd told herself, about driving to Argelès. But she'd had too much to drink. *And besides*, she thought, *if it's that bad it can wait.*

❁

Louise locked the door behind her. A dim half-light suffused the room from between latched shutters. Adèle was stretched on the bed, unclothed, watching from beneath her eyelids.

"I thought it was you," she said drowsily. "I can tell by the way you climb the stairs. It's always the same. Like you're never sure you want to reach the top."

Louise draped her handbag over the back of a chair.

"Maybe I'm not," she said, stepping into the bathroom to wash her face in cold water. The water came out tepid & she let it run, looking at her face in the mirror. "It's so hot outside. I can't stand it."

Her head swam & thought what an idiot she was, drinking in the middle of the day. But it'd been good wine. She only regretted the circumstances, though she wasn't sure what the circumstances were, exactly. She saw, coming out of the bathroom dabbing at her neck with a wet hand towel, that Adèle was frowning at her. Her shawl had slipped away & Adèle's gaze was fixed on the bruises darkening her shoulders. Then Adèle eyes clouded-over, as if the effort of concentration was too much to sustain. In a thick voice she asked:

"What happened to your arms?"

Louise crossed the room & sat on the edge of the bed. She stroked Adèle's hair.

"I'm alright. I'm glad you're here."

"So am I."

There was a vague smile on Adèle's lips. Her eyelids drooped. A barbiturate serenity settled across her face. Louise saw the bottle of the tablets lying on the bedside table. A dull heat radiated from the shuttered window. In a moment Adèle would be unconscious & she'd be left alone again. She pulled her knees up onto the bed & let her body sink upside-down beside Adèle's. Her lips brushed along the curve of Adèle's thigh. She lay her head there, gazing up at the other's face across the smooth pubic mound. She allowed her fingers to trace the line between Adèle's breasts to her naval, circling it with her fingernails. Then pressed her palm flat across the pelvis. Her hand rose very slightly & fell with Adèle's breathing.

Then her head began to spin. She shut her eyes tight. Without warning, the scene within the darkened doorway replayed itself in her mind, each detail wrenched through some inner distorting prism. Faceless assailants grappled with her thoughts, forcing their way as if through some mental *cordon sanitaire*. Her entire being seemed to contract around some dark knot of herself. She struggled to breathe. Somewhere inside, she was being forced again to undergo punishment of being that thing, that hole, receptacle, cunt. As though her sex by itself was a provocation to some narcissistic violence. For man in all his insufficiency to worship, despise, use, violate, stuff & obliterate.

She clenched her teeth. Her thighs & pelvis seemed to rigidify. All was black & then, little by little, a dull red aura coming through the darkness. Her faceless aggressors once more withdrew into the shadows. She felt Adèle's hand on her face. Gradually the tension ebbed. Adèle's hand slipped away. When she opened her eyes again, something in the way she was lying startled her. She raised her head & looked down. In her convulsions she'd bitten into Adèle's thigh. Her jaw ached. A trail of saliva joined her chin to a set of purpled indentations. A feeling of sudden grief came over her & she covered the teeth marks with her hand, wishing them undone.

Adèle lay there oblivious. Her nakedness, something perfect that'd been stupidly marred. Louise stared at the back of her hand in horror & amazement, unable to move it. Adèle's flesh seemed to radiate beneath her touch. To burn with the stigmata of her own shame, absolving her of it. *If I love you I'll only cause you pain*, she thought, gazing at the other's face distorted through her tears. But Adèle was deep in the serenity of sleep. Her breathing, a slow, unconscious rhythm.

✹

Louise smoothed her dress with the palms of her hands, regarding herself in the bathroom mirror. Hair tightly combed back, gathered behind her head, exposing a slender white neck to the light. A hint of eye-shadow & lipstick, further accentuating the natural angles of her face. Like a paler Nefertiti. Her dress was yellow, with a floral print. The bruises on her arms barely noticeable in the half-light, masked by anti-blemish cream. A voice came from the doorway.

"You're stunning," Adèle said, coiled against the doorpost, camera in hand. Still naked, her hair was tangled against her face. Louise stole a glance down her body. The bite marks were still there, only less pronounced. Adèle gave her an enigmatic look. Her left hand played across the crease of her thigh. Louise closed her eyes, keeping her mind as blank as possible. The camera whirred. She opened her eyes again, turned to consider herself in profile. Angled her hands to the light to scrutinise her nails. Another whir. She smiled weakly at Adèle's reflection in the mirror.

"I'm a wreck," she said. "When I get anxious, I bite my nails till there's nothing left. And I've been anxious since I got here."

Adèle pursed her lips at the image in the viewfinder.

"Let me help," she said.

She went back into the other room, flicking the hair from her eyes. A moment later she returned without the camera, wearing a bathrobe & carrying a makeup kit. Louise studied her as she arranged herself on the edge of the bidet.

"What're you doing?"

"Voilà!" said Adèle, holding up a sachet. "Come here."

She motioned to the toilet seat beside her & Louise sat. Half-an-hour later Louise spread her hands & gazed at the affixed nails, varnished in the same hue as her eye-shadow.

"D'you really think so?" she asked, realising at the same time she wasn't wearing her wedding ring & hadn't been all day.

"Of course. They suit you."

Adèle lent forward & kissed her lightly on the mouth, then traced a line with her index finger along Louise's bottom lip.

"I'll catch up with you on the terrace. You can see if your husband needs someone to carry him home yet."

Adèle laughed & stood up. Louise didn't laugh.

"He's not so terrible," she said, feeling depressed all of a sudden. "We shouldn't be too hard on him. His mother died when he was very young. He never knew his father."

"I daresay that can be tough on a boy his age, Louise, but isn't it time he got over it?"

"It's just that I feel sorry for him."

"You shouldn't allow yourself to be manipulated like that, playing the little woman. Let him hold his own hand."

Louise looked strangely at Adèle & Adèle, sensing she'd overstepped, lowered her eyes.

"I know it's none of my business," she said. "It's you I care about."

"I know," Louise said, touching Adèle's face. Thinking: *You have to slough off your old soul to penetrate the dark?* She said: "Soon."

27
red desert

Everything outside the frame also
becomes part of the scene...
– Arod Suliman

Three days ago, with Luce in Paris. We met at the Rostand, opposite the Luxembourg Gardens. It was overcast, the sky grey-&-white. Like an ultrasound showing no inner life. We sat at a table divided from the street by plastic sheet that kept the drizzle out. I drank three coffees to stay awake. I hadn't slept, as usual, during the sixteen-hour journey from Prague. Afterwards we saw Antonioni's *Red Desert*, with Monica Vitti & Richard Harris, in a little arthouse joint on the rue Cujas. The film was Luce's idea. Like Vitti in the film, in the scene when she first appears, Luce was wearing a green overcoat. I'd wanted her to come to Laboe. I even suggested she write an article about Ascher for *Art Press*, now she'd finally put an end to the Derain book. There was the question of Ada. She'd had a miscarriage late in her fifth month & been slow to recover. Wolf's unborn double, saved from the abortionist only to fall victim to misadventure. She was convalescing in Luce's place on Denfert Rochereau.

Wolf hadn't spoken with Ada since Prague. He'd cross the world to pay his last respects to a dead friend, but this was something else. Behind his fanaticism, there was still a little boy afraid of being left behind. When Luce asked if I'd told him, I lied. I tried to balance the reasons, though in the end there probably weren't any. After the film I invited Luce up to my room at the Trois Collèges. She shook her head, said she'd meet me for breakfast but had other engagements at the minute. I told her I'd been off the drink since Collioure. She said she was happy for me & kissed me on the cheek before leaving. I wondered what the other socalled engagements were. Is that what she'd told Ada, when she meant she was coming to see me?

Outside, at the intersection, there was a police van with half-a-dozen riot cops standing around, talking. Students were picketing the Sorbonne further down the street, though nothing seemed to be going on. For once, thinking about what I'd just told Luce, I skipped a nightcap at the bar & instead went straight to my room & took a shower. Through the bathroom window I could see into an apartment diagonally across the intersection. A dark-haired girl was standing naked in front of a mirror, applying makeup to her face. It was a strangely melancholy scene. The girl made me think of Marita. For all the times we'd fucked, I'd never seen her completely nude. The girl across the street had the same hair, the same complexion. Or at least it seemed so on that cold, drizzly Paris evening. I expected at any moment she'd turn & look out the window, & I'd see her lips forming words that'd never reach me. But she didn't. The lights went out & I was alone with my thoughts again & somehow managed to slip by them into a restless sleep.

Next morning, as agreed, Luce arrived at the hotel dining room. This time she was wearing a beige overcoat. We drank coffee & watched the students passing on the street. The cops had gone. We hardly spoke during the ride across to the station. At the Gare de l'Est, Luce waited on the platform till the train was ready to depart. She stood there the whole time with both her hands in her pockets & the coat done up, a patterned chiffon scarf around her neck. Normally she avoided farewells, but I sensed this time she was making an exception because she intended it to be for good.

What would it mean to regret nothing? To choose to return & repeat again, to the last detail, every act you'd ever committed? To lie awake in the dark the way an animal does, without the voice of conscience forever nagging at the back of your head? To listen to the night as though you were listening with your whole body? Not through the ear, but with the ear. No longer a mind detached from itself, but a palpitating body the night discerns. In which it discovers its own breathing, its rhythms, its contours.

Picture a man & a woman facing each other across a table. From a distance, it's difficult to determine the nature of the drama taking place. They seem unable to communicate. Both take turns speaking, yet their bodies seem at odds with one another. As though they're speaking two versions of the same language. Two people, or someone alone staring into a mirror, or into the dark, listening to his thoughts, to her thoughts, or to the black silence. Like being at the end of a very long question you can't remember the beginning of...

Perhaps the image doesn't belong there.

I remember something Luce said once. Or quoted to me, from the English poet William Blake. How thought alone can make monsters. And I wonder if we aren't all monsters in that case. And something Wolf said. About how no other animal is asked to form an attitude towards its own extinction. An attitude & a judgement. And lastly, there's Derain, who after all I've discovered a grudging respect for. Saying that we can only grasp within the world a truth that doesn't present itself to be seen, but which we must learn to render. Am I understanding at last? And something else the pastry chef's son said, that I take to be my own: *I can visualise the shapes I want to portray & it's these shapes that're killing me.*

28
La Lune

7:40 p.m. Hess at a table on the terrace. A half-empty bottle of Saint Dominique beside a plate of shrivelled olives & sliced baguette. The crowd along the strand. People weaving among the tables. The constant babillage. *Gimps, hustlers, hookers & stray dogs...* Hess loosening his collar. *The heat, at the end of the day. Sullen as a woman's body,* he thinks, *who's no longer desired but merely available...* Down along the water's edge a line of children stood tossing pebbles into the sea. Pebbles in fistfuls or one at a time. Their ritual seemed to protract itself for hours. Rank & file, hoisting stones into the air. The stones plucking at the grey glass surface of the water. The surface shattering & reforming & shattering again. Hess muttered to himself drunkenly: *And let him who has not sinned cast the first stone!*

In the middle of the beach, a pair of toddlers were struggling with a rock that was obviously too large. No-one paid them any attention. Their effort at first appeared doomed, but they didn't give up till the rock had at last been rolled into the water. Some weird atavism presided over the scene scene. Like crabs, those children, come out along the shore at dusk, making obeisance to the sea. Its respirations, its hungers & digestions. And as Hess struggled to keep those crab-children in focus, the thought suddenly came upon him: *I never knew when I was young. It's something you only learn about afterwards, when it's too late... I'm old,* he thought. *I've grown old.* Wise with his thirtythree years. Telling himself he'd rather blow his brains out than live till he was forty. One afterlife, he thought, was enough. Purgatory for sins committed by others before he was born. He had a sense of slowly decomposing. Sitting there in the stuporous afterglow. Feeling the flesh gradually easing away from his bones, drooping like warm tallow.

"We're all dissolving," he said aloud, half to himself, half to anybody, "into that sea of spleen."

His outburst attracted a few curious looks from the tables nearby. He turned to stare at them & they looked away.

"Escargots!" he muttered.

A family at the table immediately to his right were all gorging themselves on crème Catalane. It was like a scene from Balzac. Hess felt ill just looking at them. He leered at them, unnoticed.

"The authentic bourgeois saloperie," he snickered, pouring another glass of wine.

Mothers. Daughters. Old men. Like those ridiculous characters in novels. *L'esprit de cette bourgeoisie en vacances qui ne s'ennuie jamais dans ses rituels, parle pour passer le temps, sans se départir d'une amabilité artificielle. Revenir continuellement aux même questions, avec une naïveté mêlée d'ironie...* One of the children stuck its tongue out at him, gobs of crème Catalane hanging from its bottom lip. Hess was about to do likewise, but caught himself in time & instead shouted something at a waiter, who ignored him.

"Better to kiss a leper than to shake hands with a cretin," Hess intoned.

Who'd said that? Something he'd read once somewhere in a book by someone. Which book? Any book. What the fuck did it matter anyway? *Words, words. Why can't they just shut up?* To the amused looks from various parts of the terrace Hess responded by turning his chair noisily so as to face in the opposite direction.

✸

Luce was wearing a yellow patterned dress & her hair was knotted up behind her head. Hess caught sight of her at a distance, emerging from the crowd along the strand, down the steps & onto the path that ran between the tables two rows over. He amused himself watching her, impassively, as if she were a stranger. But his amusement was spoiled by the recognition that she actually was a stranger. Disturbed by this sudden realisation he waved anxiously at her, till he was able to catch her attention & she came over. She immediately noticed how drunk he was.

"I'm not as bad as all that," he pleaded. "It's the heat, you know."

Luce eyed the empty bottle standing on the table.

"Is this any good?"

She waved down a passing waiter to order another one.

"What a perfect evening," she said, stretching back in her chair & inhaling deeply. "Don't you love the atmosphere?"

"I loathe crowds."

"But it's different after dusk!"

"Yes, it's different I suppose."

The waiter returned with the wine, uncorked it, & stood the bottle on the table, taking the empty one with him. Luce took out a cigarette & lit it.

"Are you happy?" she asked.

"Man has been posing that question since the dawn of time."

"And has he found an answer yet?"

"I've a suspicion he's still unsure," he said, managing to pour Luce a glass of Saint Dominique without spilling, & then another for himself. "Santé! Here's to happiness."

Luce smiled at him broadly, lifting her glass to touch his.

"I'm sure you could be happy, Hess, if you wanted to."

He looked at her ironically.

"I've heard rumours to that effect."

"Ah!" she said, drawing out the sound so that it seemed to resonate with any number of possible meanings. "I'm happy, at least," she said finally, still smiling at him.

He watched Luce sip her wine, gaze turned to the sea. Her eyes glistened beneath the coloured lights. The pattern on her dress, he noticed, was of orange & red bougainvillea. As she drew on her cigarette, her breasts swelled beneath the light fabric, & the bougainvillea momentarily came alive as though something in the air had stirred them.

And am I happy? he wondered. He imagined Wolf saying something like: *You've lost your nerve.* Not knowing what to do, to think, to say, or even how to experience. Was it as bad as all that? The fine line between pain & nothingness. Squandered opportunities, wasted time. *But what if there never had been opportunities?* Hess reflected. *If it'd all been one smoke screen after another?*

"They've taken my script away," he said morosely.

"Who has?"

"The studio. They've given it to someone else."

"Can they do that?"

"They've done it."

"Is that why you're unhappy?"

"Me?" Hess attempted a laugh. "What're you talking about? You think I'm joking? I don't even have a sense of humour. See, now I'm stealing your lines."

She didn't laugh, she only looked at him, her face gone tense.

"I don't mean to be a bore. Anyway," he added, "I'm reconciled to it. More fish in the big puddle, etcetera. Live & learn. How about you? How's life treating?"

Luce finished her cigarette & stubbed it out.

"Well," she said. "I'd say well."

She took another mouthful of wine, then smiled at him again. It was a rather forced smile.

"I'm sorry about before."

"Oh," she said, raising her eyebrows as if surprised.

"I mean…"

190

"Have you been waiting here long?"

She glanced over at the belfry to check the time. It was a little before nine.

"Not long. Just getting started. I've got the whole night before me." He poured some more wine. "How's your book of books?"

Luce said something noncommittal, keeping her gaze fixed on a distant point somewhere out at sea. While she spoke Hess watched, fascinated, as a woman at a neighbouring table set to work on a seafood platter the size of a toilet seat. Her bovine face seemed to graze around the edges of a large calamari that stood in the middle of it like a marine Priapus, encinctured with raw oysters in their shells. King prawns. Green muscles. Giant sea snails. Assorted other crustaceans marinated in a piquant brownish discharge suspiciously like intestinal scoria...

Then it was Hess's turn to talk & straightaway he began to ramble. In his mind their conversation took on a completely surreal quality. He was no longer sure of who was speaking. Someone beside or behind him seemed to put the words in his mouth. Like a ventriloquist's dummy. But the things they conveyed were entirely in his head. When he looked around, nothing *out there* seemed quite as real.

A band struck up at the end of the beach, using the breakwater as a stage. It was a moody, amorous piece of jazz. Hess stared at the small crowd gathered beneath the wall to listen. His speech, already confused, became agitated. He made a sudden wild gesture, almost catching the tray of drinks a waiter was carrying between the tables. Luce gave him a startled look.

"Them, can't you hear them?"

The band. The indistinct hubbub of the terrace.

191

"No, Hess. Who're *they*?" Luce said.

"The ones who're taking me away."

"No-one's taking you away, Hess."

Hess stared at her uncomprehendingly.

"Do you want me to help you back to your room?"

"I don't know."

He stared glumly at the table cloth. Then the music got louder. He felt somebody's presence & glanced up. Standing under the coloured lights at the edge of the terrace was Ada, radiant in white. It was the first time he'd seen her without a camera. Luce was smoking a cigarette, flicking the ashes on the ground. Ada was looking at her. Slowly, as if in a dream, Luce turned to Ada & smiled.

"Shall we?"

Ada held her hand out across the table.

"D'accord, chérie."

Luce took the proffered hand & stood up. Hess was almost beside himself.

"But I have to tell you something," he blurted out, staring at his wife's fingers. There was something wrong about them.

"What is it?" Luce asked, without looking at him.

"It's about Wolf…"

Ada laughed, a slightly high-pitched laughter.

"Wolf!" she exclaimed, as if he'd said something hilarious.

The two women stepped down onto the beach, paused to remove their sandals &, arm in arm, continued to the water's edge. They stood there for a while, looking at the mooring lights reflected in the harbour. And then, holding each other, they began to dance to the slow jazz.

Hess's watched them till he was no longer able to focus their forms clearly against the falling dark. The shape of the harbour seemed to absorb them. Then everything else went out of focus too. Instinctively he drank another glass of wine, seeking that island of calm he knew lay further inside the drunkenness. He slumped in his chair & closed his eyes. When he opened them again the sky had darkened & become night. To the east, towards Perpignan, lightning flashed intermittently without sign of rain. To the west, a clear black sky. The stars flashing their anomalous Morse.

Hess finished his glass & discovered the bottle also was empty. Quite suddenly he felt very tired. Behind him the carnival lights began to sway & multiply. He pressed his hands to his temples, trying to concentrate on one single thing. Across the port, a halo of light had begun to surround the hillside. Hess fixed his attention upon it, straining to bring it into focus. But it wouldn't resolve. And then it became clear: it was the moon. He watched the yellow orb bulge out above the hillside, leering like a giant's eye from behind Fort St-Elme.

"C'est la lune!" someone behind him said.

Then there were more voices. Heads turned along the terrace to take in the spectacle.

"The full moon rises," Hess intoned, "from heaven across the world to hell. *Vom Himmel durch die Welt zur Hölle.*"

"Qu'est-ce que c'est?" voices asked.

"C'est la lune!" more cried.

La lune! The great white egg of the night. *La lune! La lune!* They stared up at it with astonishment, as if expecting it to hatch. Hess couldn't endure the noise any longer. He tossed some money on the table & staggered away from it, teetering on the terrace ledge, searching to get his bearings. The moon – yes, he could see it – was almost fully risen. Brightening the entire hillside below the fort. Lighting the wings of the old Moulin that stood above the port. *Molino de viento. Molino de aliento.* He stumbled towards it. The crowd on the terrace howled after him. *La lune! La lune!*

29
doppelgänger

No means of public life are left
which don't have, in some way or
another, the main goal of serving the
interests of capital. This also holds
true for the Left, whose activities do
not extend beyond their subscribers,
their supporters, their internal
organisation or their cadre. These
activities play themselves out in the
context of mostly private,
coincidental, personal & bourgeois
forms of communication. No
publications escape the control of
vested private interests – through
advertising – through ambitious
journalists trying to make a name for
themselves – through TV & radio –
& through the concentration of
media ownership. In the public
domain a powerful elite has the
dominant role. They divide & spread
themselves around the marketplace,
filling in market gaps & distributing
ideological content for specific
audiences...

– Ulrike Meinhof

The old house is just as I remember it. Except it's further from
the marina than I remembered. As time expands, distance
contracts. Perhaps that's it. There's a light on in one of the
upstairs windows. I have a strange urge to call out & see who it
is. I know the room, it's the one above the stairs where the settee
with patterned upholstery used to be, facing a large dressing
mirror, Venetian blinds hanging in the window. I can hear

Auntie Freude calling up the stairs. Blue house-coat & beige stockings. And the mules she wore, clacking on the floorboards. Her hair piled up on her head. Neck bare.

It hurts to picture her in a rest home, lying in a bed in a room stinking of piss. In my mind she'll always remain that most beautiful of all women wrapping me in her arms on her sagging double bed while we watched *The Bicycle Thief*. It's a disgusting euphemism, *rest home*. The degraded prelude to the eternal *requiescat*. A chemically induced easing of the soul in a tacit property-rite of euthanasia. The genteel concentration camps of advanced capitalism. There's no hope for her. Congenital dementia, they said, accelerated by years of alcoholism. What I'd never noticed it as a child. Or I'd noticed but not understood. Or I'd understood & chosen to ignore. My mother, suffered also, I'm told. They tell me I've got a fifty-fifty chance myself.

Looking at the old house, someone's dug-out the garden & lain in paving stones with a low hedge all around the yard. In my mind I see again the stagnant pond rippling with tadpoles & mosquito larvae. The colourful spiders on their webs. The rusted tricycle & the sick tree whose branches kept falling off in the wind & which had to be cut down. Like an extinct microcosm. It exists now uniquely in my memory of it. A memory I don't even want. I think of Joost's glasshouses. We've all dwelt there, in those glasshouses, with their artificial life. Blithely tossing stones till all the panes have turned to shattered glass. And the fog's crept in to suffocate the delicate roots.

❂

At last the phone rings. It's Wolf. *The ghost returns to announce itself.* Later he'll tell me how he'd just arrived in Keil, flown in late from Damascus. The connection from Berlin to Kiel-Holtenau. In half an hour his taxi will've arrived & that'll be that. The proverbial end-in-sight. All this & not a single drink. It feels strange. I've been walking around killing time, looking at the boats in the marina. Nothing's changed & yet everything's changed. I expect it's always like that. You recognise some underlying arrangement, even when the things themselves are no longer there. Something ghostly, familiar, alien, conveying the sense you don't belong. That you're a stranger to be kept at arm's length. Your motives in coming to this place treated with suspicion. As well they should be.

A pale disc of light glows through the clouds lying on the horizon over Mecklenberg Bay. The East. The sun rising in its failed Socialist Paradise. A half-tide gently rocks the boats at their moorings. The hulls tied up at the piers, butting against old rubber tyres. The streetlights have been turned off & a veil of bluishness hangs over the waterfront. A late fishing trawler chugs in the distance, sending up a faint plume of diesel exhaust as seagulls arc & veer soundlessly above.

The cigar store Indian's still there outside Wenzel's Concession, only they've changed the name. Someone called Dahlheim. We used to watch it, the woodfaced Indian, to see if it'd move. As if its stillness was a subterfuge, like the redskins in movies playing dead. Gojko Mitic in *Die Söhne der großen Bärin*. On TV in those days there'd be these re-run westerns late at night. Ford, Hawks, Peckinpah. And from time to time one of those Soviet ersatz films. *Osterns*. Yugoslavs with feathers in their hair. There was a story, that when Mitic finally got to America after the Wall came down, the Sioux made him an honorary member of their tribe.

✸

I decide to stop by the diner after all. It's just how I expected it to be. Scarred zinctop with yesterday's papers stacked at one end.

A dismal looking advert for the Sommerbühne no-one's gotten 'round to taking down, beside a stand with wilted-looking postcards of people in wicker beachchairs baking in the sun. A copy of the morning's *Kieler Nachrichten* lies on one of the stools. It beats staring out the windows into the grey. Israel still in process of withdrawing from Lebanon, a week since the blockade lifted. The socalled July War. It was supposed to've ended mid-August. UN resolution 1701.

I skim the article, but it's too depressing. Nobody's talking about the two kidnapped Israeli soldiers anymore. Meanwhile, thousands of refugees can't return because of unexploded cluster bombs. Has progress been made? I think of Wolf, his very moral sense of justification. I'm no longer able to question his outrage, even if I disagree with his motives. Is it so easy to know who's just, who's justified? Who's friend, who's foe? Do we still live in that dream where Fate only ever dooms our adversaries? Perhaps the details are arbitrary. Interchangeable. Like a film driven by internal tensions only incidentally related to the characters & plot. Is history just 24-hour news fed on a loop? Picture Lazarus, body & soul, three days on the nose & a leper to boot. Getting the glad hand at the gate & a bomb tucked inside his rags. *One hand washes the other, friend...*

I ought to laugh at myself for thinking like this. Why? Because it's true. And because we can look at the world & ourselves in it & still keep a straight face. Isn't that the real terror in our day & age? All the lost sleep of recent history won't buy a better alibi. What'll it be today? Getting blown-up by a plane kamakazied into prime Manhattan real-estate? A bomb on a London bus? On a train in Madrid? In a hotel in Armagh? In a market in Mumbai? Being kidnapped in Bogota? In Karachi? In Algiers? Being gunned-down on the street in Caracas? Bulldozed in Gaza? Tortured in Cuba? Imprisoned underground for thirteen years in Vienna? Anthraxed in Washington? Grenaded in

Kosovo? Nuked? Tsunamied? Fatwaed? Greenhouse-gassed? Ozone-depleted? Pyramid-schemed? AIDS-infected? Genetically-modified? Sweatshopped? Hormoned? Credit-maxed? Carbon-taxed? Privatised & corporatised? Phone-hacked & wire-tapped? Brainwashed? Identity-thieved? Wrongly accused? Evicted? Litigated? Salad-dressed? Having your head beaten in by your local cop? Being sold a dud battery? Missing the end-of-season sale? Getting cold feet? Losing your shirt? Not receiving an invitation? Growing tired of it all? Finding out the reasons were never the ones that mattered?

❂

I sit down & order a coffee. There's a foul taste in my mouth. It's hard to believe Wolf'll be here in less than twenty minutes. The thought of actually seeing him again makes me faintly nauseous. And I realise that while I've been walking I've been clutching the bag with Ascher in it as if he might slip away from me somehow. There're sweat-marks from the palms of my hands. Like evidence at a crime scene.

The coffee arrives & as anticipated it's undrinkable. The clock on the wall ticks very slowly. The moment of judgement approaches but not before time. It's only because of Wolf that I'm thinking like this. As if my whole existence had been dedicated to postponing precisely this moment. The way he's always threatening to return, like some obscene personal ghost. Wolf, not Ascher. To feed me my pound of flesh…

I tell myself to snap out of it. Leave some change on the counter & head back to the marina to wait. Thinking the last time I laid eyes on Ascher was '89. The Year of the Wall. We stumbled into a new decade. The decade everything ended. Our little drama no longer had a stage. What mattered anymore? Happiness? Freedom? Art? Ecstasy? The bereavement of an abolished working class? Obsolescence was the new black. The future never looked brighter.

It was the kind of thing an eleven-year-old Oswald Spengler might've dreamt up. The payoff at the end of the post-historic rainbow. Watching the closing credits scroll up on that *Weltanschauung* of pointless irrational struggle. Ready to tune in next week for the continuation. What'd Wolf hated more, the System, or the revolution against it that'd failed? He wanted to chant his magic slogans & see the whole show self-destruct. Blow itself up. Like a suicide bomb made of words.

I read somewhere that Lenin called cinema the most important of all the arts, because it was the most political & the most dynamic. It resembled, he said, the revolutionary idea in all of its facets. Something more potent than armed struggle even. But had cinema failed like revolution had failed? And what type of a film would Lenin have made anyway? *Gone with the Wind?*

❂

I wait facing the dead Indian outside Wenzel's concession. The old chief seemed bigger when I was a kid. Perhaps he just shrivelled up as the world got smaller. I want to ask him if humanity can ever be content, but it's an idiotic question. It reminds me of Nietzsche's last letters, when he wrote how he'd go around the streets tapping strangers on the shoulder, & shout at them: *Are you happy? I'm God, I made this caricature.*

Maybe Wolf had always understood this better than I did? His father died on TV news, an image disguised as truth. Where images *are* truth. It might just as well've been the Springers & Hearsts & Murdochs who'd pulled that trigger. Pimping the image naked before itself. And the darkness behind it. The conflagration of the spectacle, the laws of reason, cause & effect. Obscene, ugly, monstrous laws. Like a botched suicide.

30
The Starry Night

The distant storm moved westwards across the sea. Driven by an unshaped compulsion, Hess staggered along the darkened path that led towards the Moulin. High above it, the silhouette of Fort St-Elme stood framed in the moonlight. The storm's echo resounded across the mountainside in percussive, surreal orchestration. *Its ten thousand thunders ranged in gloom.* The path grew steeper with every step.

The Moulin, once he'd reached it, was squat & vaguely grotesque against the sky, like a dwarf's idea of a shipwreck with the sails stripped off. Behind it, a clearing opened out, ringed by pines, the moon directly above. An ancient ceremonial grove. Hess stalked from the shadows into the light, eyeing the round moon. From its low zenith it bulged unnaturally. The tops of the trees glimmered palely, like the protruding teeth of a dark devouring beast. Beyond the clearing, the path maintained its ascent, weaving the nettled undergrowth. Unsure of his bearings, Hess wandered from thicket to thicket, through unavailing gloom. Not knowing what lay ahead, he grew apprehensive of what lurked behind. Between the thunder he heard the sound of a stone being kicked. He held his breath. The sound came again, like muffled footsteps. Certain he was being followed.

Hours seemed to pass like this, struggling through the bushes, the sluiced-out ground. Lightening cast the landscape in a general metamorphosis. Black laughter. Animal danger-signals emanated from the undergrowth. *Cri cri cri cri.* Insect-voices. Toad-voices. A wounded tree-trunk oozed bloody resin. Dragon flies & oleander flies blinked s he approached. Owls. Cats.

Squirrels. *Cri cri cri.* His lungs heaved, his pursuer silently behind him. Then all of a sudden he was standing out in a clearing on the hillside. Olive groves & vineyards lay below. The path forked, turned, winding the hillside towards its invisible summit.

He leant against a rock to catch his breath. The footsteps resumed. Louder. Closer. Till they almost seemed upon him. Then they were right there, inside him. A deep, hollow beating. He closed his eyes, listened, then opened them again. The whole valley was bathed in moonlight. He looked back at where he'd come from. His pulse thumped. He barred his teeth & laughed. The dark shape following him, standing beside him, stalking ahead of him, was his shadow. Up the steep irregular incline, he stumbled on. The rustling in the ears, blood in the cerebral arteries. Like a tuning fork resonating with a wrong note. Glass stressed against glass. The fabled music of the spheres, broken by black thunder. A lunatic glass-blower's hammer & tongs working the orange orb into its final form.

As the ground levelled out, the shadows dissolved into a sort of visual disturbance. A hiatus between animate & inanimate. Upon the summit stood the fortress rock of *la Guardia.* Behind it, the black bitumened foothills of the Spanish frontier, framing a landscape whose parts had been laid blindly atop one another as though a pair of idiots had taken turns at composing it. The sky hung down like a greyish, malleable body on a gallows, one bulging moon-eye slit side to side.

Atop his mountain, Hess was perhaps closer than he ever expected to be, to those caves to which Wolf had so fervently wished humanity to return. A humanity still wondering if it'd taken God's place. *When gods die,* Nietzsche said, *they always die many kinds of death.* Thought Hess: *Man dies only once, yet resurrects himself countlessly.* He laughed aloud at his own sagacity. *The dead are more active in this world than the living. What a democracy we have in store for ourselves.*

203

A low mist had begun spreading from the valley up the hillside, as if the whole landscape was smouldering underground. The village lay in darkness. There was only the moonlight aglow upon the mist & sea. The rumbling of spent thunder. Hess teetered under a sudden fatigue. *The man on the mountain*, he thought. *An old lush.* What would Luce have thought if she could've seen him there?

"Damn her," he muttered. "Damn all of them."

He staggered backwards & fell over. The hanged man stared down at him. The fat maggoty moon. *Looks like you're fucked, old chum. They've got you by the neck. Bet you didn't expect that, eh?* He lay there considering his options. Flat on his back beside the road to nowhere. A monologue in the key of disconnect unwound inside his head. Images out of expired film stock, percolating into the night, a ghostly blob suspended in air.

"The man in the moon!" he slobbered. "Even you don't care if I live or die. And so you shouldn't. But don't expect me to."

A pair of dogs barked back & forth at one another somewhere in the valley. Hess groped his way to his feet. The place was deserted, not an audience in sight. He wished something would come along to break the tension. A stranger, to pull everything into a different perspective. *Maybe do me in*, he thought. *Put me out of my misery.* Like one of his lousy scripts. But then he reminded himself that, after all, he wasn't like Wolf. He didn't believe an empty existence could be redeemed meaning through the actions of others. *Haha.* Did he?

Up in the sky, the Dog Star constellation turned its snout westwards. Hess, with the bleakness of a man assured of his own insignificance in the greater scheme, turned also. And began to walk along the road. Following the Dog Star further into the mountains. Slowly at first & then with greater determination. Till soon, in apparent defiance of gravity, he was running. Head down. Staring at the bitumen skidding beneath him.

31
sickness

Slowly the pieces are fitting together. I have the Zen-like impression of awaiting a resolution that'll only come once I've ceased rejecting it. But it's just an impression. There'll still be other nights, other accountings. If one scene concludes it's merely so we can see where the next has already begun. The telemovie scrolls-on with its unvarying schedule of pap. Real-estate for the underinhabited mind. There, it's done. Now everything returns to what it was.

In the last entry in my notebook before Wolf's message arrived, the pattern of atonement's already there, behind the shapelessness of observations leading nowhere. Being in the midst of a situation with no delineation:

This afternoon, to dispel ghosts, I walked back along the road from Fort St-Elme to Fort Dugommier. Several of the hillsides were charred from burn-back, the smell & taste of ashes lingering in the air. I passed a grove of olive trees. The nuggety, unripe fruit & grey upwards-fanning leaves. The word "sinuosity" comes to mind. In the fields below, old vines have been pulled up by the roots & heaped in a large mound to be burned. Further on, a silhouette moves patiently among the terraces spraying younger vines with a hand-pump. Bare hands. Bare head. A stand of cork trees & wire strung on crooked wooden posts edge the winding dirt road. Below, sun-bleached

*terra cotta rooftops. Orange-blue. The still, glassy water. Once upon a time,
someone cultivated the first olive tree, the first vine. Gathered up the first
stones into hillside terraces. Tilled the dry rocky soil. Drew wine from stone.
First light. The sun warming the earth, the pine needles. Low scrub clinging
to the roadside. Yellow grass & wild barley clogging the drainage ditches.
An arbour with trees stripped of their bark by three grey donkeys penned-in
by a makeshift wire fence.*

It reminds me of another scene. A landscape of obstacles &
obstructions, bleakness & desolation. One of many similar
locations in a scenario for a film I've tried but failed to write ever
since I can remember. The scene begins with an open field of
reeds & long grass. On one side of the field, a straight dirt road
recedes towards the horizon. A stand of poplars interrupts the
uniform flatness. On the other side, a raised dyke blocks the sea
from view. As the camera advances across the field, you – the
viewer – become aware that the field's traversed by a network of
irrigation ditches. The ditches are shallow, dug from yellow clay
hardened by the sun. There's no water.

In the middle of the field, dividing it horizontally, is a low
embankment. A track runs along it between the dyke & the dirt
road. It's towards this embankment that the camera appears to
be moving. As it moves, you're aware of a voice. Speaking to
you. At least it seems to be speaking to you, since there's no-one
else. It's a slow, measured voice. Familiar. Ordinary. It's the kind
of voice you've heard before, anywhere. The kind of voice that
doesn't belong to anyone. The kind of voice you hear in dreams:

*There're many types of sickness in the world. There're the ordinary
everyday types of sickness. The life-threatening types of sickness. The species-
threatening types of sickness. There're the spiritual & physical types of
sickness. And there're the real & imaginary types of sickness. Each of us,
in one way or another, is an expression of a type of sickness...*

As the camera approaches the embankment the voice breaks
off. You suddenly rise up into the air, as if all along you'd been

hovering, floating. You're floating & looking down at what's on the other side of the embankment. You see a dried-up causeway. On the dusty bed, hundreds of people lie motionless, bodies entangled. The frame freezes. And then the eye, the camera, begins to zoom in, to hunt its prey.

The camera comes to rest in close focus on a face. A pair of eyes. The eyes open in a sudden, convulsive movement, staring up at you. And then the voice returns, as if completing a thought left hanging only a moment before, saying: *Which type of sickness are you?*

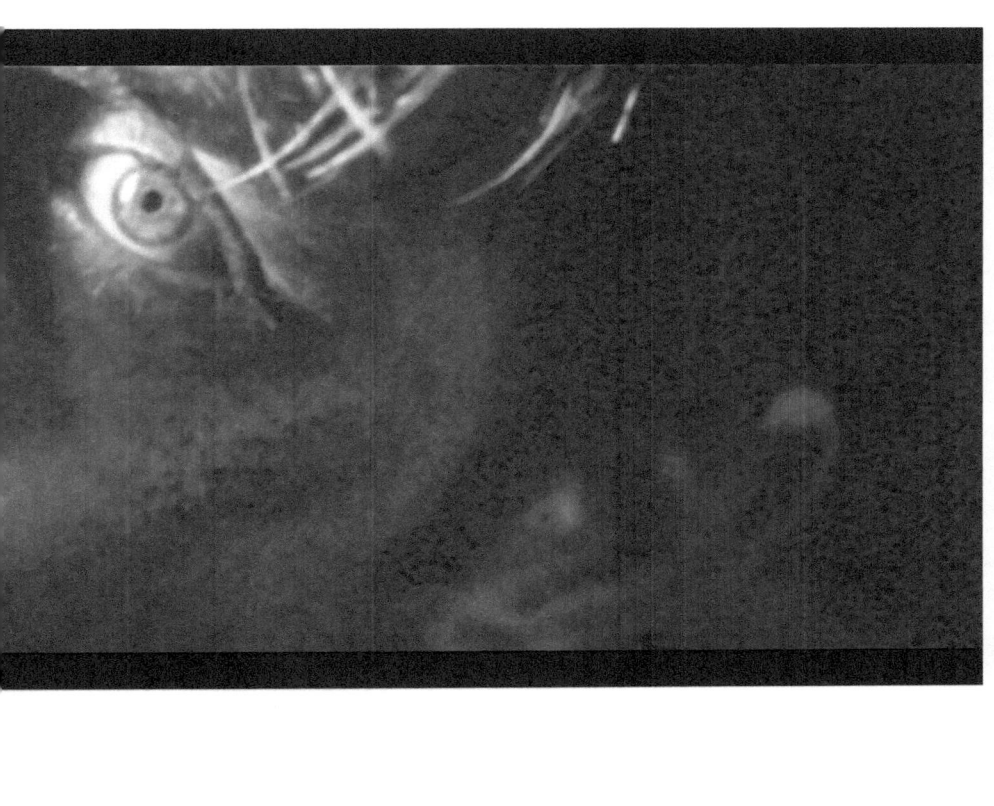

32
Gorgon's Head

In the window of the patisserie on rue de la République, someone had pasted a picture of Salvador Dalí wearing a baguette on his head. The words PAIN FRAIS, PRÊT-À-PORTER were scribbled across the top in red ink. While looking at it, Hess caught sight of his own reflection. Pale, unshaven, black around the eyes. The effort to keep himself in focus, visible in the clenched jaw, in the furrows beneath the receding hairline. He looked, he decided, like something that'd ceased to function correctly. Like that baguette on Dalí's head. A couple passed by on the pavement without paying him any attention. *Why the hell should they?* he thought. *I don't exist. I'm just a figment of a sick mind.* Overhead, a moon-marbled sky gave false intimation of approaching dawn.

The clock behind the hotel reception desk blinked, four zeroes lined up like jackpot numbers on a dud poker machine. During the night the power must've gone off. It seemed like hours navigating the stairs. When he finally got into his room he could hear voices from next door. He shoved the connecting door aside. Luce & Ada stood there like shop window mannequins. Luce, arm stiffly raised in the middle of some sort of gesture. Ada, mouth open, with her horrible little white teeth showing. They both stared at him. He realised, then, that he was ranting at the top of his lungs & stormed back out. He bolted the door behind him. *What the fuck are you doing?* There was knocking at the door. A voice said something. It sounded familiar. He sank onto the floor beside the bed, forehead pressing to the wooden boards. There were other voices, too, but soon they were all out of hearing & the darkness came over him.

✪

Sleep when it arrived, it was like being tipped over a precipice, staring at a black pit. Then he saw himself fall, arms out, body shaking like an empty fuselage at terminal velocity. Down below, the sea, indistinct, sun catching the wave-crests, white crisscrossed lines breaking the surface. Soon he could discern coastline. The blackened stumps of trees. A lagoon. He was gliding, now, low over the water towards the shore.

Then he found himself standing in the middle of a railway track. The tracks ran straight under the front door of an old frame-house. Blue tattered awnings & windows boarded-up. It looked familiar. The door stood ajar. Inside, it took time for his eyes to adjust to the gloom. Gradually shapes emerged. Walls, furniture, an empty picture frame. A stairway cut a hole in the ceiling. The stairs groaned as he climbed them.

Where they led was a room painted white. A broken TV flickered atop a cabinet. In the middle of the room a woman lay facedown on a bed, naked. The floor swayed as he crossed it. The walls rattled. The cracked windowpanes also rattled. The woman was asleep. Or dead. Or *as if* dead.

Obeying an unconscious command, Hess climbed onto the bed & lay on top of her. Her body, inert, shuddered beneath him. The whole room shuddered. He slapped the back of her head. Then slapped again. And continued slapping, with increased violence. The head twisted around unnaturally. Where the face should've been was a mirror. In it, his own eyes stared back at him, like the eyes of a madman.

Once more he was falling. Beneath him, a giant mirror. As he fell towards it, the mirror moved away. In it he could see all the dreams he'd ever had. His eyes sought to come closer, to leave the body & enter the mind's reflection. The dreams shimmered & moved like fish in water. Then without warning he was inside the mirror. Swallowed by the silver screen & now part of the film. And as he spiralled deeper in, he blinked up at the gibbous eye of a projector, a pale orb in the sky, animating the dreams through which he drifted. Like two halves of the same consciousness.

In one of those dreams Hess awoke in a sudden convulsion, the sun writhing in the sky like a Gorgon's head. He was lying on his back. Standing in a circle around him was a group of children. Something about his appearance fixated them. Looking down, he saw how his arms & legs were decomposed tentacles. While all around, a desert of black sand stretched away.

❂

The pain wouldn't subside. Hess lay there clutching his head. The orange glow of the streetlights flickered across the ceiling as a ceiling fan listlessly turned. It was no longer a purely physical pain he struggled with, but a pain emanating from the core of his being. An unfixed, shapeless pain. He struggled with it as with a demon, a blind threat.

Eventually the struggle would end. Outside, the darkness would still be there, humid, enveloping. And again, as he had the previous night, he'd imagine crossing the room to the window. He'd picture himself sniffing the air, thinking how it carried a smell of concealed rottenness. Above the rooftops, the moon would be almost full & he'd listen to the insects. But for now he remained in the grip of paralysis, tangled in sweat-sodden sheets. While the fan spun shadows in the room's chiaroscuro.

Hess stared at the spreading shape for what felt like hours, watching it teem. Whole mental dramas rehearsed themselves there. Finally, the clamour of the garbage trucks announced the coming of dawn. The shadows faded & objects advanced out of the gloom. The pain slackened its grip. Eventually it'd relent, as it always did, with the first light like a dispelled superstition. For an hour he slept, a sleep untroubled by dreams.

Just after seven, he struggled from bed & groped his way to the bathroom. Stared at his mirror-self from dark pits of eyes. He drew back his lips from his teeth in a theatrical grimace. The gums had bled. He spat carefully into the plughole, forced himself to drink a mouthful of tepid water. Back in the room he drew aside the curtains. A sky full of embers simmered above the rooftops, waiting to be stirred into life, cauterise the weak flesh. All through the night dark humours had convulsed within him. The sea – he felt it in his guts – was heaving & contracting, as if something he himself was joined to was straining to be born. Dogstar rising.

33

impunity

Man isn't a thing, but a drama...
– José Ortega y Gasset

The taxi left Wolf at the end of the Laboe marina. He was standing there, at the Taxizentrale, wearing a tracksuit top, like Rüdiger Vogler in *Wrong Move*. I can just about picture him, up on the Zugspitze, nursing his fiction about the Kind Man & the Pitiless Man. As if we'd swapped roles. The would-be auteur, trying to turn his anomie to the good, & the jejune provocateur. Like those students outside the Sorbonne, puffing on their Marlboros. Playacting. Less real than a matchbox dropped in the street. I look at Wolf standing there, but all I see is a tired adult version of the kid who used to flirt with the Latvian girls working the marina twenty-something years ago. Traded their socialist paradise for the free market. Gastarbeiters, he called them. A joke. They'd ruffle his hair & promise sweets if he went with them. The sentimental education.

As I walk towards him now I feel like I'm walking back in time. And suddenly there I am, hovering above myself like a surgeon over a patient on an operating table, about to make the decisive incision just as the patient opens his eyes & says, *I can still feel it, the anaesthetic isn't working*, though the surgeon hasn't even begun cutting yet. But even as I'm about to be cut up, dissected, anatomised, I see myself lying content & naked on a rock out in the sun. Just as I did when I was a kid. Listening to the herons & seagulls grazing the tidal flats. And there's Wolf, standing in front of me. Automatically I hold out my hand for him to shake, but he simply looks at me with dull eyes & asks:

"Is that him in the bag?"

"Yes," I say, feeling all of a sudden ashamed & letting my hand drop.

"Let's get it over & done with, then."

❂

Our last face-to-face, in Prague, before he left for Beirut. We'd been speculating about what'd happen if the Yanks went ahead & bombed Iran. WMDs. Secret nuclear programmes. Iraq all over again. The peaceniks had been demonstrating outside the US embassy. Cops took photographs of everyone in the crowd. The benevolent police state at work. The crackdown came afterwards. Dawn raids on outer-suburban squats. Arrests, beatings, seizures. Kids with dreadlocks, hoods, Doc Martens, red anarchist flags. The media put the scare into the general public about lunatic fringe elements, home-grown terrorist cells, bad apples. Whole swathes of emergency legislation got trolleyed-out, to protect your average law-abiding Joe. Enough paper to start a nice Reichstag fire. If you'd put it in a film, no-one would've believed it.

"Protest never serves the interests it's supposed to," Wolf said. "Unless the power-struggle's on the *inside*. You don't get to the top by hand-wringing & coming on all teary-eyed over a bit of social injustice. Think about it. Millions on the streets in London. More in New York than during Vietnam. Mass protest all over Europe. Net result? Nada. What do they expect? If the System took them seriously, they'd all be shot. Realpolitik's fought in cold blood, not with mantras & Buddhist olios. Even terrorism, socalled, is just a shadow of what governments & corporations & the IMF & Big Media are prepared to do every day of the week to maintain the status quo."

You get the picture. Like listening to a human agitprop machine. An android in the service of the Revolution. I stared at him but couldn't think of anything to say. Maybe he was right.

"The peaceniks are giving it to them for free. Non-violent protest? The little guy against the big evil empire? Bullshit. Maybe that stuff sells Coca-Cola, but as far as politics goes, it's for the birds."

I thought of Nietzsche. It isn't permission man seeks, but impunity. Wolf read my mind.

"Only God has impunity…"

"…?"

"D'you know what divine justice is? Divine justice is Abraham on the mountain, ready to stick the knife in. God's Oedipus complex. What was going through Abe's head at that moment, d'you think? *This'll hurt me more than it'll hurt you, kid, but hey, I got no choice. For the greater love of necessity. Amen.* And if the son dares to raise a hand against ol' Pop? Sacrilege! Society'd sooner murder its own children than permit a single prerogative of its just & beneficent self to be put in question. That's the real meaning of status quo. D'you know if you're oppressed or not? Perhaps we should consider ourselves lucky."

"Things could be a hell of a lot worse…"

"You mean there's no bogey on the mountain top?"

"What do I know? I've never seen him. Have you seen him? Give him my regards next time."

"You've got no class."

"Sure I do. The film industry proletariat. But I still need a producer who'll take my script."

"You need to start writing the truth."

Maybe I ought to've been flattered, that he still expected better of me.

"It's a dog's dinner, friend. *Canis manducare canem.* You dress it up in a modicum of civil liberty & what d'you get? The masochism of democracy. Nice, isn't, to have something to aspire to?" Then he quoted his beloved Meinhof at nauseating length, word for word, as if he'd spent his whole life memorising it.

"…?"

"D'you believe one day there'll be peace everlasting? You don't need a roadmap to know which way the wind blows, Joe. Think, in only two hundred years you get from Washington crossing the Delaware to Woodstock. The Yanks think they can teach us all about revolution because they had the 60s. Fuck that."

❁

I used to think Wolf had a sense of humour, but getting intimate with the real world's a serious business, I suppose. Reason maybe I got washed-up in fantasy land. But there was something funny about listening to Wolf, like he was trying to flog a dead horse an insurance policy. *Abraham? Washington? Mickey Mouse?* Change the names, what odds did it make? Comic book agents of the quid pro quo. *Like the Holy Fathers of the bloodiest marches in history, exalting murderous generalities…* But all generalities are murderous.

The Americans have a saying. *World order isn't inevitable, it's only necessary.* And they're right. Philosophy's all well & good, but it only gives you a theory of liberty after it's been traded off on the Marketplace. The only revolutionary force in the world today's corporate capitalism. Even Marx saw that one coming. Why resist? Besides, who'd be willing to go to the necessary lengths? As usual, Wolf had the last word on that, too:

"Better to be comforted knowing that in time the System'll devour itself," he said, "like a hungry dog. The vultures & ants will inherit the rest. There'll be food for all. Justice will've been seen to be done. It'll be a long slow lesson in enlightenment. D'you think it'd be worth the wait?"

At least his sense of irony hadn't completely deserted him.

"Humanity," he made an expansive benevolent gesture, "just isn't prepared to do without its illusions. Maybe it couldn't, even if it wanted to. Man's not a rational animal, despite what they say. On an evolutionary scale, rationality's for termites. Civilisation, my friend, is driven by a hopeless romanticism. Which is why we cling to the belief that things could be better. Only we can't keep even this basic sentiment in perspective. Our greatest claim to fame's to've turned the mere fact of ourselves into something worthy of divine creation. We'll suffer almost anything because – despite overwhelming evidence to the contrary – we really do believe destiny wears a human face."

Fast-forward to the present. For a moment I perceive the whole panorama of the human predicament – Goethe & Space Invaders – & somehow Wolf & I making it through to the next level, with the extra game & time bonus, but still playing for different stakes. Then suddenly we're standing between a pair of dunes, children again. And Wolf, holding a dead rabbit by the ears, pissing on a mound of freshly turned sand. With Ascher's face visible were the piss has washed the sand away…

I don't ask about what happened in Lebanon. I've seen enough in the papers. We walk in silence down along a concrete footpath across the sand dunes towards the beach. There's a faint drizzle. I'm only wearing a suit jacket, collar turned up, shoulders already soaked-through. We stop for a moment at a rise from which it's possible to see the water. We scan the fields for the back of Ascher's old house. It isn't there. A whole new development of holiday bungalows has been laid out across the once-vacant land, right up to the dunes. Piles of brick & wooden frames stand out of the drizzle.

It's too late, I think. *Everything's gone. There's no reason to've come back here.* Wolf seems to guess my thoughts. He buries his hands deeper in the pockets of his tracksuit.

"It's good you came," he says. "You've been away too long. You need to see how things have changed. It has a sobering effect, I feel. It's important to be reminded we're not children anymore. All of humanity's lost its innocence. Even us."

It's the first thing he's actually said to me since we left the Marina.

❂

You can tell from the waterline the tide's coming in. A dull sheet of grey water conceals almost the entire stretch of black sand fanning out from the breach. My watch says nine o'clock but the clouds still cast a heavy gloom over everything. There's a boy standing at the far end of the beach, where the caves are, throwing a stick to a black Labrador that bounds back & forth tirelessly through the shallow water. We walk along the beach in the opposite direction, towards the pine grove. I try to think of something to say. When we stop, just below the place where we used to undress & hang our clothes in the branches, I tell Wolf about Ada's child. Maybe he knows already, but his face shows nothing & he says nothing.

I should let it go, but an idea keeps trying to piece itself together in the back of my head. Something he'd told me. Something about the child's great hate of what's gnawing at the mother's womb. The desire to castrate the father & eviscerate the mother. To be the sole one. I think how all that'd ever truly belonged to us were terrible memories of no-one being there. Perhaps that's what Nietzsche called the death of God. How could we've become fathers in our turn?

I open the carry-bag & Wolf reaches in & takes out the parcel that's inside. Marita wrapped the ashes in so much newspaper & packing tape that in the end Wolf has to tear it open. A fine grey dust sprays out of one end, scattering over the water. He doesn't wait to say anything but simply shakes the parcel violently in the air, pausing from time to time to wrench the opening further apart. The whole ceremony seems empty & somehow bereft. And yet because of that, it expresses everything. The dismay. The abandonment. The gaping futility.

This, then, is how I finally picture Wolf. Standing in the drizzle on that shale-strewn beach. A wad of torn newspaper in his hand. And a thin paste of grey ash smeared over hands, sleeves, trouser legs. Staring angrily at the water. And all the while the incoming sea, like an unbodied intelligence, somehow fixing & shaping & holding everything in place.

Collioure – Prague – Laboe
July 2006, August 2008, November 2012